MAIGRET
IN EXILE

GEORGES SIMENON

MAIGRET IN EXILE

Translated by Eileen Ellenbogen

A Harvest/HBJ Book
A Helen and Kurt Wolff Book
Harcourt Brace Jovanovich, Publishers
SAN DIEGO   NEW YORK   LONDON

Printed in the United States of America

Library of Congress Cataloging in Publication Data

Simenon, Georges, 1903-
Maigret in exile.

Translation of La maison du juge.
"A Helen and Kurt Wolff book."
I. Title.
PZ3.S5892Maeko   [PQ2637.I53]   843'.9'12   78-13771
ISBN 0-15-655136-5

First Harvest/HBJ edition 1982
A B C D E F G H I J

MAIGRET
IN EXILE

1

The Customs Officer's Wife

•

"Fifty-six, fifty-seven, fifty-eight . . ." counted Maigret. Not that he cared a rap about the score. He was keeping count mechanically, his mind vacant, his eyelids drooping.

"Sixty-one, sixty-two . . ."

He glanced briefly out onto the square. The lower halves of the windows of the Café Francais were of frosted glass. Through the clear glass at the top there was nothing to see but the bare branches of trees, and rain and yet more rain.

"Eighty-three, eighty-four . . ."

There he stood, holding his billiard cue, seeing himself reflected in the multiple mirrors on the walls of the café.

And Monsieur Le Flem, the proprietor, in silence, carried on with his break, looking completely relaxed, as if everything was just as it should be. He moved from one side of the green table to the other, bent over it, straightened up, absently watched the run of the balls.

"A hundred and twenty-two, a hundred and twenty-three . . ."

The room was vast. Near the window a middle-aged servant sat sewing. That was all. Just the three of them. And a cat stretched out in front of the stove.

And it was barely three o'clock. And this was only the thirteenth of January. Maigret noted the date on the big calendar pinned up behind the cash desk. And things had been going on in this way for three whole months! And . . .

He had not uttered a word of complaint. Not even Madame Maigret knew why he had fallen into disfavor, and been appointed to the post of divisional superintendent in Luçon. Such matters pertained to the seamy side of his calling, and were no concern of anyone else.

Madame Maigret was there, too, in their rented apartment over a music shop, and there had already been some unpleasantness with the landlady because . . . Oh, well, no matter!

"Where do we stop?" asked Monsieur Le Flem, simply to ascertain how many more points he needed to score.

"At a hundred and fifty."

Maigret smoked his pipe in long, leisurely puffs. Get on with it. A hundred and forty-seven, a hundred and forty-eight, a hundred and forty-nine, a hundred and fifty! The balls rolled to a stop on the table, the white one discolored to a liverish yellow and the red to a feverish pink. They returned their cues to the rack. Monsieur Le Flem went across to the beer pump and dispensed two halves, slicing off the surplus froth with a wooden knife.

"Cheers!"

What else was there to say?

"It's still raining."

Maigret put on his overcoat, rammed his bowler hat well down over his eyes, and then, with his hands in his pockets, plunged into the slanting rain and tramped along the streets of the little town.

Presently, he opened the door of his office, its walls plastered with official circulars. The smell of Inspector Méjat's brilliantine assailed his nostrils. He wrinkled his nose. It was a sickly smell, which even the persistent fumes of his pipe could not dispel.

A little old woman in an old-fashioned bonnet, with a wrinkled face, was seated on a chair, clutching the handle of a huge, dripping umbrella of the sort commonly to be seen in the Vendée region. A long trickle of water had already collected on the wooden floor, as if some dog had forgotten its manners.

"What's going on?" growled Maigret, pushing through the barrier that divided the office in half, and towering over the Inspector, who was his sole assistant.

"It's for you. She won't talk to anyone but you."

"What do you mean, for me? Did she ask for me by name?"

"She asked for Chief Superintendent Maigret."

The old woman, aware that she was being discussed, pursed her lips with an air of conscious dignity. Maigret, from force of habit, riffled through the papers on his desk before even taking off his coat. It was all routine stuff—a group of Poles that needed watching, failure to produce identity cards, contravention of restricted travel orders. . . .

"At your service, madame. Please don't get up. But first, I'd be obliged if you'd tell me who gave you my name?"

"My husband, Chief Superintendent . . . Justin Hulot . . . I'm sure you'll remember him when you see him. His is a face one doesn't readily forget. . . . He was customs officer at Concarneau when you were there on a case. . . . He read about your transfer to Luçon in the paper. Yesterday, when he saw that the corpse was still there in the bedroom, he told me I must . . ."

"Sorry to interrupt, but what corpse would that be?"

"The one in the Judge's bedroom."

A cool customer indeed! Maigret observed her with mild interest, little dreaming that he was destined to become much

5

more intimately acquainted with this sixty-four-year-old woman, Adine Hulot by name, and that he, like everyone else hereabouts, would soon be calling her Didine.

"To begin with, I should explain that my husband is now retired, which is how we come to be living in my own part of the country, in the village of l'Aiguillon. I have a little house near the harbor, which was left to me by my late uncle. . . . I suppose you've never heard of l'Aiguillon? . . .

"I thought not. And that means you won't find it easy to understand. . . . But who else is there for me to turn to? Certainly not the local policeman, who, besides being drunk from morning to night, can't stand the sight of us. Nor the Mayor, who cares for nothing but his mussels . . ."

"His mussels?" echoed Maigret.

"He's a mussel-gatherer, the same as my late uncle and most other people in l'Aiguillon. He cultivates mussels."

Inspector Méjat, the silly fool, saw fit at this point to snicker and look knowing. Maigret quelled him with a frosty look.

"You were saying, dear lady . . ."

She needed no encouragement. She was taking her time. She, too, had responded with a cold stare to Méjat's uncalled-for snicker.

"It's a respectable calling, like any other."

"Of course. Go on."

"L'Aiguillon is quite a small community, made up of some twenty families, situated in the vicinity of the harbor. The Judge lives in the biggest house in the village."

"One moment. Who is this Judge?"

"His name is Forlacroix. He was formerly a magistrate at Versailles. If you want my opinion, I suspect he got into some kind of trouble, and it wouldn't surprise me to learn that he had to be dismissed from the public service."

6

She certainly had it in for the Judge. Diminutive though she was, and old and wrinkled, she was not afraid to speak her mind about people.

"Tell me about this corpse. The Judge's, is it?"

"No such luck! His kind never gets bumped off."

Capital! That put Maigret firmly in his place. Méjat spluttered into his handkerchief.

"You'll have to let me tell my story in my own way, or I'll get into a muddle. . . . What date is it today? The thirteenth . . . Good God! And to think it never struck me . . ."

Hurriedly, she touched wood and crossed herself.

"It was the day before yesterday, so it must have been the eleventh. The night before that, they'd had people in. . . ."

"Who are 'they'?"

"The Forlacroixs. Doctor Brénéol and his wife and daughter were there. . . . Or, I should say his wife's daughter . . . because . . . But I won't go into that; it would take too long. In short, they were entertaining a few friends, as they do regularly once a fortnight. They play cards until about midnight, and then all hell breaks loose, with all the cars revving up at once."

"You appear to be very well informed about what goes on in your neighbors' house."

"Our house, or, rather, my late uncle's house, backs onto theirs. So, whether we like it or not . . ."

It would have done Madame Maigret's heart good to see the flicker of interest in the Chief Superintendent's eyes. Characteristically, he was taking repeated little quick puffs at his pipe. He went across to the stove, poked in it, and remained standing with his back to the fire.

"Now then, about this corpse . . ."

"The following morning . . . The eleventh I said it was, didn't I? . . . The following morning, my husband took advan-

7

tage of the fine weather to prune the apple trees. I held the ladder for him. Perched up there, he could see over the wall. He was just on a level with the second floor of the Judge's house. One of the windows was open.... And, all of a sudden, there he was, clambering down, and this is what he said to me:

" 'Didine . . .' " My name is Adine, but everyone calls me Didine. 'Didine,' he said to me, 'there's someone lying on the floor in the bedroom.'

" 'Lying on the floor?' I repeated after him, scarcely able to believe my ears. 'Why should anyone be lying on the floor when there are goodness knows how many beds in the house?'

" 'Well, that's how it is.... I'm going up to have another look.'

"He went up and he came down.... Now there's a man who never touches strong drink, and when he says a thing is so . . . And besides, he's a thinker. It's not for nothing that he was thirty-five years in the public service.

"All that day, I could see he was deep in thought. After lunch, he went out as usual for his little walk. He stopped at the Hôtel du Port....

" 'Now here's an odd thing,' he said when he got back. 'No stranger seems to have arrived in the village yesterday, either on the bus or by car.'

"It bothered him, you see. He asked me to hold the ladder for him again. And afterward, he told me that the man was still lying there on the floor....

"That night, he kept watch until all the lights were out."

"What lights?"

"The lights in the Judge's house. I should explain that they never close the shutters at the back. They think no one can see in. Well, anyhow, the Judge went into the bedroom and stayed there for quite some time.

"My husband got dressed again and rushed outside. . . ."

"What for?"

"In case it might have occurred to the Judge to dump the body in the water . . . But he was soon back.

" 'The tide is out,' he said. 'He'd be up to his neck in mud.' "

"Next day . . ."

Maigret was dumbfounded. He had come across a good many oddities in the course of his career, but this elderly couple, the retired customs officer and his Didine, spying on the Judge in his home, from their little cottage, holding the ladder for each other . . . !

"Next day, the body was still there, lying in exactly the same position."

She looked at Maigret, as if to say:

So we were right all along, you see!

"My husband kept watch on the house all that day. At two o'clock the Judge went out for his usual walk, accompanied by his daughter."

"Ah! So the Judge has a daughter, has he?"

"I'll tell you about her some other time. *There*'s another odd fish for you. And there's a son, too. . . . But it's all too involved. . . . If that assistant of yours over there will be so good as to stop snickering into his handkerchief, I will proceed."

Méjat had asked for that one.

"High tide last night was at nine-twenty-six. There was still nothing he could do, don't you see? There are always people roaming around up to midnight. And after midnight there wouldn't be enough water. . . . So we decided, my husband and I, that I should come and see you, leaving him to keep an eye on things. I caught the nine o'clock bus. This gentleman here was just trying to get rid of me. . . . My husband's instructions were:

9

" 'Tell the Chief Superintendent that you were sent by the customs officer from Concarneau, the one with the slight squint. Explain to him that I had a good look at the corpse through my field glasses, and that the man is a complete stranger to the district. Tell him there's a stain on the floor, and that I'm convinced that it's blood.' "

"One moment," interposed Maigret. "When does the next bus leave for l'Aiguillon?"

"The last one has already left."

"How far away is it, Méjat?"

Méjat consulted the map of the district, which was pinned on the wall.

"About thirty kilometers."

"Telephone for a taxi."

For all he knew, Didine and her customs officer were a pair of nuts. No matter! At the very worst, he would have to pay for the taxi out of his own pocket.

"I'd be obliged if you'd stop the taxi and let me out before we reach the harbor, so that I won't be seen in your company. It will be best if we pretend we haven't met. They're a suspicious lot in l'Aiguillon. You can stay at the Hôtel du Port. It's the better of the two hotels. And almost the whole village congregates there after supper, so you'll be able to look them over. And if you can get them to put you in the room overlooking the ballroom extension, you'll be able to see the Judge's house."

"Let my wife know, will you, Méjat."

Night had fallen, and it seemed as if the waters had covered the face of the earth. The old woman was enjoying the comforts of the taxi, which had formerly been a private limousine. In particular, she was thrilled with the cut-glass flower vase and the interior electric-light fixture.

"Who would have thought it! The rich have all the luck."

Marshes; extensive acres of flat land intersected by canals; here and there a low-lying farm, a shack, or *cabane,* to use the local dialect term, or a stack of dried, pancakelike cow pats stored for fuel.

In Maigret's heart something stirred faintly. Could it be hope? He dared not yield to it yet. Was it possible that here, in the very heart of the Vendée, the scene of his exile, fate was about to present him with . . . ?

"I was forgetting. . . . High tide tonight will be at ten-fifty-one."

It was really astonishing the way the old girl could pinpoint the time to the minute.

"If he wants to get rid of the body, this will be his opportunity. Over the river Lay, which flows into the harbor, there is a bridge. At eleven, my husband will take up his watch on that bridge. If you want to talk to him . . ."

She tapped on the glass partition.

"Let me out here. I'll walk the rest of the way."

And she disappeared into the watery darkness, her umbrella billowing out like a balloon. Presently the taxi drew up outside the Hôtel du Port and Maigret got out.

"Do you want me to wait?"

"No. You'd better go back to Luçon."

Men in blue, fishermen or mussel-gatherers; varnished deal tables scattered around, with carafes of white and rosé wine. Then a kitchen. Then a ballroom, used only on Sundays. A smell of fresh paint and varnish. White walls. A stripped pine roof. A rickety little staircase more suited to a doll's house. A bedroom, also white, a painted iron bedstead, chintz curtains.

"Is that the Judge's house over there?" he inquired of the little chambermaid. There was light showing, through a skylight above the staircase, he presumed.

It was suggested that he be served in the dining room reserved for summer visitors, but he chose to eat in the bar. He was regaled with oysters, mussels, and shrimp, followed by fish and leg of lamb. He listened to the men talking among themselves, in their thick regional accents, about matters relating to the sea, and, in particular, about mussels, a subject that was a closed book to Maigret.

"Have you seen any strangers around here lately?"

"Not for the past week . . . I should say, not for the past couple of days. . . . No. Let me think. It was three days ago. A man came in on the bus. He stopped here to say that he'd be back for dinner, but he never showed up."

Maigret stumbled about in a great pile of rubbish, iron bars, lobster pots, bits of wire, crates, and oyster shells. There were shacks all along the waterfront, used as storage sheds by the mussel-gatherers. A deserted village built of wood. At two-minute intervals came the boom of a foghorn, located, so he had been told, on Pointe des Baleines, the tip of the Ile de Ré across the harbor.

To add confusion, the watery sky was intermittently crisscrossed by beams from two or three nearby lighthouses.

There was the murmur of flowing water, as waves drove inshore against the current of the little river, which increased their volume. Soon—at ten-fifty-one precisely, if the old woman was to be believed—it would be high tide. Against the wall of a shack a pair of lovers, oblivious of the rain, clung together, mouth to mouth, wordless, motionless.

He made for the bridge, an immensely long wooden structure, just wide enough to take a single line of traffic. He could faintly make out the shadowy outlines of masts and fishing boats bobbing on the tide. Behind him could be seen the lights of the hotel from which he had just come, and, barely a hundred yards away, two lighted windows, the windows of the Judge's house.

"Is that you, Chief Superintendent?"

He gave a start. The man was so close that he had almost bumped into him. Maigret noticed that he had a pronounced squint.

"I'm Justin Hulot. . . . My wife told me . . . I've been here for the past hour, in case he took it into his head . . ."

The rain was cold. An icy wind was blowing in from the sea. The grating of chains could be heard. Invisible in the darkness, the nocturnal life of the waterfront was in full spate.

"I must bring you up to date on events. . . . At three o'clock, when I went up the ladder, the corpse was still there. At four o'clock, I decided to take one last look before it got dark. . . . Well, I found that it was no longer there. He must have taken it downstairs. I guess he wanted it handy near the door, to save time when the opportune moment came. . . . I can't imagine how he'll manage to carry it. The Judge is even smaller and skinnier than I am. . . . Well, actually he's about the same build and weight as my wife. The corpse, on the other hand . . . Shh!"

Someone was abroad in the dark. One after another, the planks of the bridge could be heard to creak. When there was no further risk of being overheard, the customs officer went on:

"On the other side of the bridge lies the village of La Faute. . . . Well, you can scarcely call it a village, really, or even a hamlet. It's just a cluster of little bungalows for renting to summer visitors. You'll see for yourself by daylight. . . . I've discovered one thing that may interest you, and that is that on the night of the bridge party Albert called to see his father. . . . Watch out!"

It was the lovers this time, who had moved to within earshot, and were leaning on the parapet of the bridge, gazing into the water. Maigret's feet were frozen. Water had seeped in through the seams of his shoes. The former customs officer, he noticed, was wearing rubber boots.

"It's a three-foot-six tide. . . . At six o'clock tomorrow morning, you'll see them all going out to the mussel beds."

He spoke in hushed tones, as if in church. It was slightly ludicrous, and yet at the same time somehow a little creepy. Maigret could not help wondering whether he would not have felt more in his element back there in Lucon playing cards in the Café Français with his regular cronies, the proprietor, the doctor, and the owner of the hardware store, with that senile old fool Memimot watching over their shoulders and nodding and shaking his head at every card on the table.

"My wife is keeping watch on the back door."

So the old woman was still an active partner.

"You never know. . . . He might decide to get out his car and dump the corpse farther afield."

The corpse! The corpse! Did any such corpse really exist?

His third pipe . . . His fourth pipe . . . From time to time, the door of the hotel opened and shut. Distant footsteps and voices could be heard. Then the lights went out. A rowboat glided under the bridge.

"That'll be old Bariteau, going out to lay his eel traps. He won't be back for at least a couple of hours."

How could old Bariteau possibly find his bearings on a night as dark as this? It was a mystery. One could feel the sea, very close at hand now, at the mouth of the channel. One could breathe it in. It was rising, ineluctably engulfing the outflow of the river.

Maigret experienced a sudden aberration. He could not have explained why at this particular moment his mind should have veered toward the recent amalgamation of the Police Judiciaire and the Sûreté Générale, with its attendant

14

disruptions which . . . Luçon! They had shunted him off to Lucon, where . . .

"Look over there!"

Agitated, the former customs officer gripped him by the arm.

No, really! It was beyond belief. The thought of those two old people . . . Didine holding the ladder . . . The field glasses . . . The tide tables . . .

"They've switched off the lights."

Well, what of it? Was it to be wondered at, at this hour, that the lights had gone out in the Judge's house?

Whatever he might think, Maigret was careful nevertheless to walk on tiptoe, so that the planks of the bridge would not creak. That wretched foghorn, mooing like a hoarse cow!

The water was lapping almost at the base of the wooden shacks. His foot struck a battered lobster pot.

"Shh!"

And then, as they watched, the Judge's front door swung open.

There appeared on the threshold a spry little man, who glanced to the right and the left and then returned indoors.

A few seconds later, that which had seemed incredible to Maigret happened. The little man reappeared, bent double this time, dragging a long bundle through the mud.

It must have been heavy. He was barely a few feet from the house when he had to pause for breath. The front door had been left open. He had some twenty or thirty yards to go to reach the sea.

"Heave!"

The sound came to them as a heavy sigh. They could almost feel his muscles strained to the limit. It was still raining. Through the sleeve of his thick overcoat, Maigret could feel the convulsive clenching of the customs officer's hand.

"You see!"

Yes, indeed! It had all happened exactly as the old woman had predicted, as the former customs officer had predicted. There could be no doubt as to the identity of the little man. It was Judge Forlacroix, and that bundle he was dragging through the mud was, unquestionably, the lifeless body of a man.

2

"Pardon me, old man . . ."

•

The fact that the Judge was unaware of being watched gave a dreamlike quality to the scene. He believed himself to be alone in that dark, empty place. From time to time, he was momentarily touched by the beam from a lighthouse, which revealed an old raincoat, a felt hat. Maigret even caught a glimpse of a cigarette between his lips, which had been extinguished by the rain.

They were now scarcely four feet apart. The Chief Superintendent and Didine's husband were standing near a shed, not unlike a sentry box. They made no attempt to avoid being seen. The only reason the Judge had not spotted them was that his attention was engaged elsewhere. The Judge, poor man, was in deep trouble. The bundle he was dragging along the ground had caught in a rope, which was strung out along the quayside about ten inches above the ground. He had somehow to pull it through underneath. He set about it clumsily. It was plain to see that he was unused to heavy manual labor. He was sweating, and kept wiping his forehead with his hand.

It was at this point that Maigret, quite without any conscious volition or plan, said simply:

"Pardon me, old man . . ."

17

The Judge turned his head and saw the two men, the towering figure of Maigret and the diminutive customs officer. It was too dark. It was impossible to discern the expression on his face. A few seconds went by. It seemed an eternity. Then a voice spoke, a somewhat quavering voice surely.

"Who are you?"

"Chief Superintendent Maigret."

He stepped forward, but still could not see the man's face clearly.

His feet were almost touching the corpse, which appeared to be wrapped in sacking. Why on earth, at such a moment, should the Judge have responded by exclaiming in a tone of astonishment, tempered by esteem:

"Maigret of the Police Judiciaire?"

All around them were people asleep in their houses. Old Bariteau, out there in the clamorous night, was searching for the deepest pools, in which to lay his eel traps.

"Maybe it's all for the best. . . ."

It was the Judge speaking.

"Would you care to come back to the house?"

He began walking away, apparently forgetting his bundle. Everything around them was so oppressively still that they felt as if the whole scene were being enacted in slow motion.

"Ought we not perhaps to take the body with us?" suggested the Judge, ruefully.

And he bent down. Maigret went to his assistance. The door was not shut. The customs officer stopped on the threshold, and Forlacroix, who had not recognized him, wondered whether or not he was going in.

"Thanks for your help, Hulot," said Maigret. "I'll see you in the morning. Meanwhile, I'd appreciate it if you'd keep all this to yourself. Have you a telephone, Monsieur Forlacroix?"

"Yes, but we're disconnected after nine o'clock."

"One moment, Hulot. Would you be so good as to make a call for me from the post office? The number is Lucon two three. It's a hotel. Ask to speak to Inspector Méjat, and tell him I want him to join me here as soon as he can."

So! Now there were only the two of them, face to face in the hallway, the Judge having switched on the light. He removed his dripping hat and raincoat. The sense of mystery that had pervaded the night was dispelled. What he could see, now that there was light, was a slightly built little man, with neat features, his face framed by long, very silky fair hair streaked with gray, which might almost have been a wig.

He looked down at his hands, which were filthy, and then at the bundle. Maigret saw that the body was wrapped in two coal sacks, one over the head and torso, the other over the legs. The two sacks had been clumsily sewn together with string.

"Would you like to see him right away?"

"Who is he?" asked Maigret.

"I haven't the least idea. Do please take off your coat, and follow me."

He wiped his hands on his handkerchief, opened a door, switched on another light, and stood waiting for Maigret to join him on the threshold of a spacious room, at the end of which was a fireplace with a crackling log fire.

This pleasantly warm, well-lit, tastefully furnished, tidy room was the last thing Maigret was expecting to see at that moment. The ceiling was of oak beams, which made it seem lower than it was, the more so since there were two steps leading down from the doorway into the room. The floor was of white tiles, with two or three rugs scattered about. And all along the white walls were bookcases filled with books, thousands of them.

19

"Take a seat, Chief Superintendent. If I remember right, you like a good fire."

More books on an antique table. An armchair on each side of the hearth. It was almost beyond belief that just outside the door, sewn up in a couple of coal sacks . . .

"What a stroke of luck for me to have run into a man like you. Though I don't quite see . . . I understood you were in Paris and . . ."

"I've been posted to Luçon."

"All the better for me. If I'd had to resort to the local police, I very much doubt if I'd have been able to make myself understood. . . . Allow me."

On a sixteenth-century sideboard stood a cut-glass decanter and glasses on a silver tray. They flashed and glittered magnificently under an artfully positioned spotlight. The whole atmosphere was one of serene refinement and comfort. The Judge brought the tray over to Maigret.

"Allow me to pour you a glass of Armagnac. . . . By the way, I almost forgot to ask . . . How on earth did that dreadful cross-eyed customs fellow come to be mixed up in . . . ?"

And it was at this point that Maigret suddenly appreciated how matters really stood. He had a vivid picture of himself ensconced in his armchair, his legs stretched out to the fire, his glass of Armagnac cradled in the palm of his hand. It was brought home to him that it was not he who was doing the talking, asking the questions, but this self-possessed, shrewd little man who, only a few minutes earlier, had been dragging a corpse toward the sea.

"Forgive me, Monsieur Forlacroix, but I really think you owe it to me to answer a few questions."

The Judge turned and looked at him, with an expression of mingled surprise and reproach in his periwinkle-blue eyes, as if to say:

Questions? What for? I expected better things of *you*. Oh, well! Have it your own way.

But, in fact, he said nothing. He merely cocked his head slightly to one side, the better to hear. He was all polite attention. Maigret recognized the mannerism as an indication that he was a little hard of hearing.

"You assured me just now that this . . . this man was a stranger to you."

Heavens, this was awkward. It was a straightforward question, but in these delightful surroundings it seemed somehow indelicate.

"I swear to you, I don't know him from Adam."

"In that case, why . . . ?"

It had to be said. Get on with it. Maigret felt like screwing up his eyes, as if he were about to swallow a bitter pill.

"Why did you kill him?"

He looked at the Judge, whose face once again expressed mingled surprise and reproach.

"But I didn't kill him, Chief Superintendent! Good heavens! Why on earth should I want to kill a total stranger, a man whom I never saw alive? I realize that it's hard to swallow, but I feel sure that a man of your experience must see that I am telling the truth."

And the trouble was that Maigret was already convinced of it! This house, silent but for the crackling of logs and the distant murmur of the sea, had put a kind of spell on him.

"With your permission, I will describe events as they occurred. A little more Armagnac? An old friend of mine, who for many years was the public prosecutor in Versailles, sends it to me from his estate in the Gers region."

"You yourself formerly lived in Versailles, did you not?"

"I spent the greater part of my life there. It's a delightful town. It still retains a flavor of the golden age of Louis XIV, and in my opinion you would have to go far to find a community more civilized, in the traditional sense of the word. Our little group . . ."

He made a sweeping gesture with his hand, as if to banish all such nostalgic irrelevancies.

"No matter . . . It was . . . Let me think . . . It was last Tuesday . . ."

"Tuesday the tenth," specified Maigret. "You were entertaining friends, I believe."

The Judge's lips twitched.

"You are well informed, I see. . . . Hulot was with you just now. And I daresay you have also met Didine. She knows more than I do about what goes on in my house."

A sudden thought struck Maigret. He looked about him with a feeling that there was something missing in the household.

"Have you no servants?" he asked, in some surprise.

"None living in. An old woman and her daughter, who live in the village, come in every morning, and leave as soon as they've cleared away the dinner at night. . . . Anyway, about Tuesday . . . My friends came to spend the evening with me, as they do regularly once a fortnight. Doctor Brénéol, who lives about a mile away, and his wife and Francoise . . ."

"Francoise being Madame Brénéol's daughter?"

"That's right. By her first marriage. Not that it matters, except, of course, to Brénéol."

A faint smile flitted across his face.

"The Marsacs, who live in the village of Saint-Michel-en-l'Hermitage, arrived a little later. We played bridge. . . ."

"Was your daughter also present?"

His glance wavered. He hesitated, then, looking a little pensive, said:

"No. She was in bed."

"Where is she now?"

"In bed."

"Didn't she hear anything?"

"Nothing. I was careful to make as little noise as possible. Well, to revert to Tuesday, the party broke up around about midnight."

"And then you had another visitor," said Maigret, turning toward the door. "Your son."

"Yes, Albert did come to see me. He stayed only a few minutes."

"Does your son not live with you?"

"He lives near the town hall. . . . My son and I have very little in common. My son is a mussel-gatherer. I daresay you have already discovered that mussel farming is the principal local industry."

"Would it be indiscreet to ask for what purpose your son visited you in the middle of the night?"

The Judge gazed into his glass. There was a brief silence. Then he exclaimed:

"Yes, it would."

And he waited.

"Did your son go up to the next floor?"

"He was already there when I went upstairs."

"On his way to see his sister, I suppose?"

"No . . . He didn't see her."

"How do you know?"

"Because—I may as well tell you, because if I don't someone else will—I make a habit of locking my daughter in her room every night. . . . Let's say she's given to sleepwalking."

"What was your son doing up there?"

"Waiting for me, since I was entertaining friends downstairs. He was sitting on the top step. We exchanged a few words."

"On the stairs?"

The Judge nodded. Surely they were entering a world of

fantasy? Maigret drained his glass in one gulp, and Forla-croix refilled it.

"I went downstairs again to bolt the door. Then I read for a little while and went to bed. Next morning, I went up to the fruit loft to look for . . . To tell the truth, I don't remember what I was looking for. . . . We call the room the fruit loft, since it's mostly used to store fruit, but we keep all sorts of other things up there as well. It's more of a general store-room really. . . . There was a man lying on the floor. A man whom I had never seen before. He was dead. His skull had been bashed in by what you people call a 'blunt instrument.' I searched through his pockets. . . . Presently, I'll show you what I found. . . . But there was no wallet. Not a single clue to his identity, no papers, nothing."

"What I don't understand . . ." began Maigret.

"I know! And that is what I find so hard to explain. I didn't call the police. I kept the body here in my house for three days. I waited until the tide was favorable, and then slunk out furtively in the middle of the night, intending to get rid of it. . . . Like a murderer. All the same, I am telling you the exact truth. I did not kill that man. I had no reason to do so. I have absolutely no idea what he was doing in my house. I don't know whether he entered it alive, or was brought here after his death."

He fell silent. Maigret could hear once again the distant lowing of the foghorn. There were boats out there at sea, and fishermen hauling in nets teeming with fish. Had Hulot, the customs officer, managed to get through on the telephone? If so, Méjat—what a thoroughly uncongenial fellow, with his hair all stuck together with brilliantine—must be clambering hurriedly into his clothes. He was fond of boasting of his success with women. Had one of his latest conquests been sharing his bed tonight?

24

"Well," murmured Maigret, with a sigh—the heat of the room was making him feel more and more drowsy—"it won't be plain sailing, by any means."

"I'm afraid you're right. With things as they were—the man being already dead, I mean—it would have been better . . ."

He did not complete the sentence. Instead, he crossed over to the window. It would have been better if the dead man had been carried out to sea on the receding tide, and had never been heard of again. Maigret stirred himself. He flexed one leg and then the other, and eventually managed to heave himself out of the depths of the armchair. In doing so, he would not have been surprised if he had hit his head against the rafters.

"Anyway, I think I ought to take a look at him."

It was hard to resist the charm of this low-ceilinged, well-appointed, cozy room, with its beguiling atmosphere of order and harmony. He looked up at the ceiling. What was she like, this girl who had to be locked in her room every night?

"We could take him into the laundryroom," suggested the little Judge. "It's just across the hall."

Now, both were taking care to avoid getting dirt on themselves. They were no longer outdoors in the rain-sodden night. They had reverted to being civilized men.

The laundryroom was a vast place, with a red-tiled floor. There were wires strung across it, on which clothes and linen were hanging up to dry.

"Have you any scissors?" growled Maigret, prodding the two sacks, from which water, blackened with coal dust, was trickling.

The Judge, unable to find any scissors, came back bearing a kitchen knife. The furnace was turned down. It was cold. Maigret's wet fingers were turning red.

It was a most extraordinary thing, but the element of

tragedy was entirely missing. The Judge evinced no revulsion at the prospect of looking once again upon the face of the man whom he had sewn into the sacks. Maigret was wearing his most stubborn and grumpy expression, but, truth to tell, he was reveling, with almost sensual enjoyment, in this mystery which fate had landed in his lap, and, of all places, in Lucon, the scene of his exile and disgrace. It was as if a sea lion, after ages of captivity as a circus performer, were suddenly to find itself back in the glacial waters of the Arctic.

When was the last time he had entered a house, as he had just done, with a view to drinking in the atmosphere, wandering from room to room, plodding and patient, until all its secrets, and those of the people who lived in it, were finally revealed to him?

Not to mention Didine Hulot and her customs officer. And the Judge's son, who had sat waiting for his father at the top of the stairs in the middle of the night.

And now this other character. The victim. What would he learn about him, once these filthy sacks were removed?

At one point, the scene almost degenerated into farce. He was prepared for anything, except the unbelievable sight that actually met his eyes. For, when the sack covering the upper part of the body was stripped off, and the face of the victim was revealed, it proved to be a face as black as night. Needless to say, this was due to the coal dust. It was only to be expected. Yet the two men looked at one another for an instant, both with the same thought in mind: for a brief second they were prey to the outlandish delusion that they were in the presence of a Negro.

"Could you get me some water and a cloth?"

The tap gushed noisily. When the sound ceased, Maigret cocked his head on one side, listening. There was another sound to be heard, outside, that of a car engine. A door

26

slammed. Suddenly a bell shrilled loudly in the hall. Méjat was certainly making his presence known.

"Where is the Chief Superintendent?"

There he was, facing him. The Inspector's nose was red, and a loose strand of hair hung down over his forehead.

"I hope I haven't kept you waiting too long. Am I to tell the taxi to wait, Chief? Was all that about a stiff really true? What's become of the old madwoman?"

Not only were his person and his clothing permeated with the cold, dank air of the night, but also he exuded, with his thick regional accent, a kind of coarseness which polluted the atmosphere. The quietness and restraint that had hitherto prevailed were dispelled. Méjat, however, was impervious to such subtleties of perception.

"Have you identified him, Chief?"

"I don't know a damn thing!"

The words escaped Maigret involuntarily, surprising even himself. It was an expression that had often been forced from him in the past, when he was floundering in a sea of confusion in an exceptionally difficult case, and some idiot like Méjat . . .

"My God! That's some crack he got on his head!"

The Judge and Maigret exchanged glances, both wishing that the peaceful, almost intimate atmosphere that had prevailed until now could be restored. As for Méjat, he was rummaging in the dead man's pockets, where, needless to say, he found nothing.

"How old would you say he was, Chief? I'd put him at about forty. Any identifying marks on his clothing? Do you want me to undress him?"

"Go ahead. Undress him."

Maigret, for his part, filled his pipe and began roaming in circles in the laundryroom, mumbling to himself under his breath.

"I'll have to call the Public Prosecutor at La Roche-sur-Yon. I wonder what he'll decide. . . ."

And the Judge, standing there facing him, suddenly said, with a perfectly straight face, apparently quite unaware of the ludicrousness of his words:

"It would be *disastrous* to send me to prison."

This was the last straw. Maigret blew up:

"See here, Your Honor, Judge Forlacroix . . . I don't suppose it has occurred to you that it was *disastrous* for this man here to have been clubbed to death and laid out on these cold tiles. . . . I'll bet you haven't given a thought, either, to the *disastrous* consequences for his wife and children, if any, and God knows who else, who are at present wondering what on earth can have become of him. I would also point out that the most disastrous thing of all would be to keep them in ignorance forever, just because of someone who will go to any lengths to avoid being involved."

Even the sacred obligations of hospitality were forgotten. He had been plied with the finest Armagnac, warmed to the core of his being by a fragrant log fire, filled for an hour with a soothing sense of well-being, and, for thanks, he had turned fiercely upon his host, wearing the implacable face of Maigret of the Quai des Orfèvres.

Mild-mannered Judge Forlacroix looked at him reproachfully, but said nothing.

"There's a label in the jacket!" exclaimed Méjat in triumph. "Let me see . . . Pa . . . Pa . . . Pana . . ."

"Panama," growled Maigret, snatching the jacket out of his hands. "That's a great help, I must say. A gentleman whose clothes were made in the Republic of Panama! Why not China, while he was about it?"

It was impossible to get the shoes off the man's feet without cutting through the laces. This task also fell to Méjat.

28

And this young man, so fastidious in his dress, so forthcoming with the ladies, set about it no less matter-of-factly than if he were at his desk writing a report, spelling out all the proper names in capitals, as was his invariable wont.

"The shoes come from the Boulevard des Capucines in Paris. The heels are already slightly worn, which suggests to me that he's had them for a month at least. Where do you think he comes from, Chief? A Frenchman, would you say? That would be my guess. A respectable sort of man. Not a manual worker. Take a look at his hands. . . ."

They had both completely forgotten about the waiting taxi, and the driver striding up and down outside to keep warm. Suddenly, the door burst open. There appeared at the far end of the hall a man as tall and heavily built as Maigret himself. He was wearing high rubber boots which reached to his thighs, a voluminous oilskin jacket with, it could be guessed, several thick sweaters underneath, and a sou'wester on his head.

He came forward mistrustfully. He looked Maigret up and down, and subjected Méjat to the same piercing scrutiny. Then he bent down to look at the body, and finally fixed his gaze upon the little Judge.

"What's going on?" he snarled suspiciously, almost threateningly.

Forlacroix turned to Maigret.

"My son . . ." he said. "I'd be obliged if you would explain to him . . ."

He then made haste, with little teetering steps, to proceed from the laundryroom to the low-ceilinged library, where he had originally entertained the Chief Superintendent.

"What is going on?" repeated the young man, this time addressing himself to Maigret. "Who is this man? Who killed him? You're a policeman, aren't you? When I saw a car parked outside the house . . ."

It was now five o'clock in the morning. Albert Forlacroix had been on his way to the mussel beds when he had seen the car.

"The driver told me he had brought a police inspector here from Lucon. . . ."

Suddenly he frowned.

"My sister . . . what has he done to my sister?"

He was so obviously deeply worried that Maigret was alarmed. Was it possible . . . ? While the pair of them, he and Forlacroix, had been relaxing in their deep armchairs, in front of the crackling log fire . . .

"Now you mention it, I should like to see your sister," he said in a changed voice. "Have you the key to her room?"

By way of reply, the young man merely pointed to his massive shoulder.

"Méjat . . . you wait down here."

Their footsteps rang out on the stairs, and then on the floor of a long, winding corridor.

"This is it. Stand back, if you please."

And Albert Forlacroix hurled himself at the door.

3

Airaud's Footprints

It was an extraordinary moment, and its flavor was to remain with Maigret ever after. First of all, the weariness at the end of a long night, and then the pervasive smell of damp wool. The unfamiliar and seemingly endless corridor. The renewed sound of the foghorn. Just as Albert Forlacroix was launching his assault on the door, Maigret glanced sideways toward the stairs, and saw that the Judge had crept up on silent feet to join them. Behind him, in the stairwell, Méjat's face came into view.

The door yielded, and the young giant, thrust forward by his own momentum, was propelled into the very middle of the room.

It was all so unexpected. No one could have foreseen how it would be.

The room was lit by a table lamp with a finely pleated pink silk shade. In a Louis XVI bed lay—or, rather, sat, for she was propped up on one elbow—a young girl, and as she turned to look toward the door, one of her firm, plump breasts slipped out of her nightdress.

Maigret would not have called her a beauty. Her face was too broad, her forehead too low, and her nose too childish. But her full lips were ripe and juicy, and her eyes enormous.

Had she switched on the light on hearing noises in the corridor? Had she been asleep? It was impossible to tell. She did not seem much surprised at the sight of Maigret's massive bulk in the doorway, and her brother in rubber boots standing in the middle of her bedroom.

She merely asked, in a low, composed voice:

"What's the matter, Albert?"

Her father, though keeping out of sight, had moved close enough to the door to hear her. Maigret was feeling uncomfortable. He could not take his eyes off the girl's naked breast, and, at the same time, was conscious that the young man had noted this. True, it did not seem to bother Albert, who was peering suspiciously about him. There was a second door in the room, and presently Albert went across and opened it.

Was it intuition? At any rate, Maigret felt certain that beyond that door lay the so-called fruit loft. He went over to it.

"What are you looking for?" he asked.

No answer other than a dirty look. Then suddenly Albert Forlacroix bent down. On the floor leading from the bedroom to the fruit loft there were faint footprints to be seen, the track of a man's shoes in muddy outline, and the mud still slightly damp.

"Who's there?"

Albert strode across to the window of the fruit loft. It had been left slightly open, and cold air was blowing into the room.

Maigret returned to the bedroom. The girl was propped up in bed as before, and she had made no attempt to cover her naked breast. On the evidence, it must be presumed that last night, possibly while Maigret was actually in the house, there had been a man in this same room, in this same bed.

Albert crossed the bedroom with long strides and went out. Maigret followed him. The Judge, waiting in the corridor, murmured:

"I shan't be able to lock the door now. . . ."

His son shrugged indifferently, as if it were no concern of his, and went downstairs, with Maigret close on his heels.

"Méjat!"

"Yes, Chief."

"I want you to keep watch on the house. . . . From the outside."

He recovered his coat and hat, which were hanging on a hook in the hall. It was still quite dark, but there was a good deal of activity going on outside, where a hubbub of voices and scufflings could be heard.

"When I asked you just now whether you knew the name of the intruder, you didn't answer. Can you say who he is?"

The little customs officer, looking thoroughly put out, was lurking outside. Maigret pretended not to see him.

As for Albert, he was in no hurry to give information. A very odd young man.

"Can I go to work now? Or are you intending to arrest me?"

"By all means, go to work. . . . Unless there's anything you want to tell me . . . About that man whose footprints you saw in your sister's bedroom . . ."

At this, Albert stopped dead, and laid his hand on Maigret's shoulder. They had reached the water's edge. The tide was going out fast, leaving behind a tract of blistered mud. A group of men and women, all wearing breeches and rubber boots, were loading empty baskets into flat boats, which they propelled with poles.

"The man? See there . . . That's the one."

Albert pointed to a young man almost as tall and brawny as himself, and dressed as he was, who, having helped an old woman into her boat, was pushing it out with a pole.

"Airaud is his name . . . Marcel Airaud."

And so saying, he went into one of the sheds, from which he soon re-emerged carrying a load of baskets.

The chambermaid at the Hôtel du Port was already busy, sluicing and scrubbing the tiled floor of the bar, when Maigret came in the door.

"Where on earth have you been?" she exclaimed in amazement. "Have you been up all night?"

He sat down beside the stove, and ordered coffee, bread, sausage, and cheese. And only then, comfortably installed on the padded bench, did he ask, between mouthfuls:

"Do you know anyone by the name of Airaud?"

"Marcel, d'you mean?" she replied, with so much feeling that he looked at her with closer attention.

"Marcel Airaud, yes."

"He's a local boy. . . . Why do you ask?"

One thing was plain at any rate. The young man meant something to her.

"A mussel-gatherer? Is he married?"

"Not on your life!"

"Is he engaged?"

"Why ask me?"

"No particular reason . . . I got the impression that he was hanging around the Judge's daughter."

"That's a lie, for a start!" she exclaimed between clenched teeth. "Others, maybe. And what's more, they don't have to hang around, either, or hang back, for that matter, because that girl, if you really want to know, is a . . . a . . ."

She was groping for the most offensive word she could think of, but what she eventually came out with was harmless enough.

"A nothing . . . Everyone knows that. . . . And if her brother had kept on bashing every man she invited into her bedroom . . ."

"Are there so many?"

"Practically the whole village! And then there was that time when she ran away to Poitiers . . . When they finally caught up with her, she was in a rare old state! If anyone is suggesting that Marcel and she . . ."

"I'd be obliged if you'd pour me some more coffee. Oh, and one more thing: that man who arrived by bus on Tuesday . . . what time did he get here?"

"He was on the four-thirty bus."

"Did he leave right away?"

"He just popped in to say that he'd be back for dinner, and then he made off toward the bridge. . . . I don't know. . . . It was already dark by then."

"Would you recognize him if I showed you a photograph?"

"I might, yes."

"Oh, well, it's time I got some sleep."

She stared at him in amazement.

"Let's see now . . . It's six o'clock. . . . Please wake me at eight with some very strong coffee. . . . You won't let me down, will you, my dear? You're not too angry with me because of what I said about Marcel, I hope?"

"What's it got to do with me?"

He slept soundly. It was an inestimable gift, this capacity to fall asleep anywhere, any time, and thus shelve his preoccupations from one minute to the next.

And when the girl, whose name was Thérèse, woke him with a pot of steaming coffee, a pleasant surprise awaited him. The entire face of things had changed. The sun was streaming in through the window. The room was filled with that multitude of tiny sounds which make up the hubbub of daily life.

"I'd be much obliged, my dear, if you would bring me up some soap. And if there's a safety razor to be had hereabouts, would you buy me one, and a shaving brush at the same time?"

In the interval, he leaned out of the window, drinking in the cold tangy air, like fresh water from the spring. So this was the harbor which by night had seemed so black and muddy. And over there was the Judge's house. And the sheds along the waterfront.

The scene before him filled him with delighted astonishment. The shacks, for instance, were painted in bright colors, white, blue, and green. The Judge's house was pure white, roofed in tiles of a subtle rose color. It was a very old house, to which many features had been added over the centuries. It was, for instance, surprising to discover that there was a spacious terrace beneath the window of the fruit loft, enclosed by a balustrade, with a huge green pottery urn at each corner.

And below, beyond the garden fence, was a little one-story cottage, also white, consisting, no doubt, of no more than two rooms. It had its own tiny garden, with an apple tree, against which leaned a ladder. And surely that was Didine herself on the porch, wearing a white kerchief, with her hands folded on her stomach, looking up at Maigret's window?

The mussel-gatherers were already returning home. Twenty boats, thirty boats, odd-looking flat punts known locally as *acons,* docked alongside the quay, and basket upon basket of blue-black mussels was loaded into great, rumbling trucks.

"The only razor I could get was a special offer at three francs fifty, but the man in the shop says . . ."

Well, special offer or not, it would have to do. Maigret did not feel in the least sleepy. He was as fresh as if he had spent the whole night in his own bed. What about a drop of white wine in the bar before going out? Well, why not?

"Would you like me to clean your shoes?"

Yes, indeed. Away with the mud. He wanted everything

clean and neat. And, catching sight of Inspector Méjat in the distance looking like a bedraggled cockerel drying its feathers in the sun, he could not help smiling.

"Any new developments, son?"

"None, Chief . . . Two women turned up, one old, one young. The charwomen, I suppose. What's more, as you can see . . ."

The three windows on the ground floor were open. They were the windows of the library, where Maigret and the Judge had sat by the fire for part of the night. An old woman wearing a white kerchief was shaking the rugs out of a window, releasing a cloud of fine gilded dust into the sunlight.

"What about the Judge?"

"No sign of him . . . Or of the young lady . . . Unlike that pest of a fellow over there, who never stops talking."

Maigret followed his pointing finger, and saw his friend the customs officer, whose squint was even more pronounced in the sunlight than it had been the night before. He was eagerly awaiting a summons from Maigret. The slightest sign would have brought him running.

"Wait here till I get back. I won't be long."

"Would you mind if I just slipped away for a cup of coffee?"

No sooner asked than granted. Maigret was in his most benign mood. Presently, he made his way to the police station, and introduced himself to the sergeant.

"First of all, I'll need to use your telephone. Would you get me the Public Prosecutor's office at La Roche-sur-Yon?"

The Prosecutor had not yet arrived. His deputy listened as Maigret made his report, and agreed to take the necessary steps. Next, he rang Lucon, and then made two or three other calls.

Well! Things were on the move. In spite of everything, Maigret had somehow managed to start the machine rolling.

Naturally, he felt a pang of nostalgia. In Paris, he would have had his whole trusted team to call upcn, splendid fellows, who were so familiar with his methods that they scarcely needed instructions: Lucas, recently promoted to inspector, Janvier, Torrence, and all the boys in Criminal Records and Forensics . . .

Here, he had to wait until midday before the photographer arrived, and the policeman detailed to watch the Judge's house glared so ferociously at all who came near that the café on the corner was soon buzzing with speculation as to what could be amiss.

Maigret rang the bell. The old woman opened the door.

"I'll go and see if His Honor is . . ."

"Show him in, Elisa."

He was in the big room, with everything about him in perfect order, and the sun streaming in through the three windows.

"I've brought a photographer. You have left the corpse undisturbed in the laundryroom, I trust?"

"I'll give you the key. I locked the door to keep the women out."

"Don't they know?"

"Not yet. I thought it wiser."

"Is your daughter up yet?"

What a question! As if Maigret could not hear her playing the piano upstairs.

"Is she still in the dark, too?"

"Absolutely."

In all his experience, Maigret doubted if he had ever encountered such stubborn imperturbability.

Here was a man of great refinement, a cultured, peaceable man, who, after an evening of bridge, finding his giant of a son sitting at the top of his staircase, reacted as if it were the most natural thing in the world.

And the following morning, he opened a door, to discover the dead body of a man, a man who had been murdered!

Still he remained unmoved, mentioning it to no one, going out for his usual walk in the company of his daughter.

Then followed the waiting for a favorable tide, the sewing of the body into sacks. Then . . .

The arrival of the police. His son irrupting onto the scene in a highly excitable state. The breaking down of the daughter's bedroom door. The footprints, indicating that a man had spent part of the night in that room.

Still the Judge remained unperturbed. The charwomen arrived at their usual hour, and quietly went about their daily business of cleaning the house. The girl with the naked breast sat at her piano, playing. Her father did no more than lock the door of the laundryroom where the corpse lay. . . .

The photographer set to work, and the Judge watched him as if there were nothing in the least strange about propping up a dead man in a sitting position, and trying to make him look as lifelike as possible.

"I should warn you," said Maigret gruffly, "that the Public Prosecutor's deputy will be arriving about three this afternoon. I'd be grateful if you would remain indoors until he gets here. And that goes for Mademoiselle Forlacroix, too."

Well, well, how odd that sounded! It was hard to think of the girl he had seen in bed with one breast exposed as "Mademoiselle Forlacroix." Was this perhaps because a man had left muddy footprints in her bedroom?

"May I ask if my son has said anything to you, Chief Superintendent? Would you care for a glass of port?"

"No, thanks . . . Your son merely pointed out a man by the name of Marcel Airaud. Do you know him?"

The Judge blinked, and drew in his breath.

"So you, too, suspect this Marcel of being the man in your daughter's bedroom?"

39

A low murmur, scarcely more than a whisper.

"I don't know."

The door of the library stood open. Logs blazed in the grate.

"Come in here a moment, will you?"

It was an appeal from the heart. The photographer was left outside.

"You do understand, don't you?"

Maigret said nothing. The whole situation made him feel thoroughly uncomfortable, especially in the presence of the girl's father.

"It was on her account that I left Versailles and came to live here in this house, which has belonged to my family for generations, and where we used occasionally to spend a month or so in the summer."

"How old was she then?"

"Sixteen. The doctors warned me that her attacks were likely to recur more and more frequently as she grew older. . . . Sometimes she is perfectly normal."

He looked away. Then, with a shrug:

"I didn't tell you all this at first, because I was hoping . . . I don't really know what I was hoping for. . . . Now do you see why it would have been better if the body had been swept out to sea? Everyone will say . . . God only knows what they will dream up! Not to mention that fool Albert."

"What was he doing here that night?"

Too late. The Judge's emotional outburst was spent. Just for a second or two, it had seemed as if he were about to let himself go, and take Maigret into his confidence.

Had Maigret phrased the question too bluntly?

The Judge's cold gaze was upon him. His pale eyes, in the sunlight, seemed almost colorless.

"No! It wasn't about that. . . . It's of no importance. . . .

40

Are you sure you won't take a glass of port? A Portuguese friend of mine . . ."

One of his friends sent him Armagnac, another port. It was as if his only concern was to surround himself with every refinement of gracious living.

Through the gap in the curtains, he caught sight of the policeman pacing up and down outside. With a nervous little laugh, he asked:

"Is he there on my account?"

"You know I have no choice in the matter."

He sighed and then, rather unexpectedly, said:

"It's all very regrettable, Chief Superintendent! Oh, well . . ."

The rippling notes of the piano could be heard above their heads, and Chopin's harmonies seemed admirably in keeping with the atmosphere of this civilized gentleman's residence, where the tenor of life ought to have been so smooth.

"See you later," snapped Maigret abruptly, firmly resisting the temptation to remain.

The Hôtel du Port was crowded with men back from the mussel beds. Who had been spreading the word? At any rate, all eyes were focused on Maigret as he sat down at a table with Méjat and ordered lunch.

The blue denim overalls of the men, streaked with rain and sea water, presented a rich variety of shades. The little servant girl, Thérèse, seemed agitated, and Maigret, following her glance, caught sight of Marcel Airaud drinking *vin rosé* among a group of men.

He was a young man of about twenty-five, slow-moving and placid, thickset and heavy, as they all were, especially in their high boots.

The hubbub of loud voices had ceased. All the men in the room were looking at Maigret. Then they drank from their mugs, wiped their mouths, and tried to think of something to say, anything to break the awkward silence.

One of the older men made the first move:

"Better be getting home to lunch, or the old lady will be furious."

Then, one by one, the others dispersed.

Marcel was among the last remaining at the bar, leaning on his elbow, with his cheek resting on his open palm. Thérèse came up to Maigret and asked:

"Do you like *mouclade?*"

"What is it?"

"Mussels cooked in cream. It's a local specialty."

"I can't stomach anything with cream," declared Méjat.

Marcel waited until she had gone, and then came up to Maigret's table. He drew up a rush-seated chair and, touching his cap, sat down astride it.

"I should like a word with you, Chief Superintendent, sir."

There was no servility in his manner, nor any bravado. He was completely at ease.

"How do you know who I am?"

The young man shrugged.

"One hears things. Ever since we got back from work, tongues have been wagging."

The room was empty now except for themselves and a couple of fishermen at a corner table some way off, trying to catch what was being said. The clatter of plates could be heard in the kitchen.

"Is it true that there is a murdered man in the Judge's house?"

Under the table, Méjat nudged Maigret's knee with his own. Maigret, with his mouth full, raised his head and calmly looked the young man full in the face. Marcel's glance did not waver.

"It is."

"In the fruit loft?"

And now there were tiny beads of dewy moisture on the young man's upper lip.

"Are you familiar with the fruit loft?"

He did not reply, but glanced uneasily at Thérèse, who had just reappeared carrying a steaming tureen of *mouclade*.

"When did it happen?"

"Let me first put a question to you. What time did you arrive home last night? You live with your mother, isn't that so?"

"What has Albert been saying?"

"I'm asking the questions."

"It was barely midnight."

"Do you always leave the Judge's house as early as that?"

Another uneasy glance, this time toward the kitchen, into which Thérèse had just disappeared.

"It depends. . . ."

It was a great shame to have to discuss such things while eating the *mouclade,* which was a masterpiece of culinary art. Almost without thinking, Maigret strove to identify a flavor of . . . Now, what on earth could it be? The merest hint . . . the lightest touch of . . .

"What about Tuesday?" he asked.

"I wasn't there on Tuesday."

Maigret frowned, froze for a second in an attitude of abstraction, and then suddenly burst out in triumph.

"Curry! I bet you anything you like there's a touch of curry in it."

"Don't you believe me?"

"About Tuesday? My dear fellow, I haven't the least idea. How can I possibly tell at this stage?"

"I swear to you . . ."

Maigret wanted to believe him, just as he wanted to believe the Judge. Just as, instinctively, he couldn't help believing Albert.

Which didn't alter the fact that the corpse could not have got there by itself.

4

Official Proceedings

•

All in all, Maigret had no cause for complaint. Things had worked out very well, splendidly, in fact, and when the business was concluded, Monsieur Bourdeille-Jaminet had condescended to murmur a few languid words of congratulation.

It was Maigret who had fixed upon the town hall, on the grounds that the police station was altogether too gloomy and smelled of moldy leather, cabbage soup, and unwashed children. The council chamber of the town hall was spacious, freshly whitewashed, and dazzlingly clean. There was a flag in a corner, a bust of the Republic on the chimneypiece, and a pile of social-security books on the table, which was covered with green baize.

The dignitaries arrived in two cars, led by the Public Prosecutor, Monsieur Bourdeille-Jaminet, who was so tall that it was a wonder he could see his own feet. Next came his deputy, followed by an examining magistrate, whose name Maigret did not catch, and then a clerk, the police surgeon, and a local police officer.

A detachment of police had also arrived from Lucon, and these had seen fit to form a cordon in the street, thus ensuring that crowds would gather, even if they were wholly ignorant of what was afoot.

The corpse was already there, in the courtyard. The police surgeon had obtained permission to work in the open air. Trestle tables, normally used for banquets, had been brought out. After some delay, Doctor Brénéol had arrived, looking extremely agitated. He was distantly related to the Public Prosecutor. The two men exchanged courtesies, and fell into conversation about the estate of a female cousin several times removed.

Everyone was smoking. Through the glass door could be seen the ballroom, still festive with paper decorations left over from the last party, and with benches set at intervals along the walls for the chaperones.

"Forgive me, gentlemen . . . My dear fellow, permit me to . . ."

The medical men in the courtyard. The legal dignitaries in the council chamber, the clerk almost hidden behind a pile of papers. As for the Mayor, he stood waiting in the doorway looking important, and chatting with a police sergeant.

At one point, Maigret really began to wonder whether they would ever get down to business, so little concerned with the central drama did everyone appear to be. The Judge was rambling on about some duck shoot in which he had taken part the previous winter at l'Aiguillon Point.

"Suppose you and I make a start," suggested Maigret to the clerk.

He began dictating in a low voice, almost in a whisper, so as not to disturb anyone. Had there been any new developments since the morning? Nothing much, really, except that Thérèse had identified the corpse as the man who had got off the bus on Tuesday. The bus conductor had confirmed the identification, but could not recall whether the man had joined the bus at Luçon or Triaize.

Photographs of the dead man had been widely circulated.

46

Every policeman had one. They had been shown to all the bar and inn keepers round about. Tomorrow, they would be in all the morning papers. In other words, the usual routine inquiries were under way.

"Are you going to treat us to some interesting revelations, Chief Superintendent?" asked the Public Prosecutor jocularly, as if he were a schoolmaster encouraging a pupil.

The medical men, inured to their grisly work, washed their hands in the fountain behind the public library, and joined the others in the council chamber.

The murder weapon, as expected, was identified as a "blunt instrument." A very severe blow to the head. The skull had been cracked open. The internal organs would be examined later. . . .

A healthy, strapping young man . . . The liver slightly enlarged. Obviously the deceased had enjoyed good food and drink. . . .

"You may take my word for it, Monsieur le Procureur, my good friend Forlacroix, with whom I was playing bridge on the night in question, had nothing whatever to do with this murder. . . ."

"Shall we go, gentlemen?"

It was not worth bothering with cars for so short a journey, so they walked in procession. Followed by the whole population of the village! And, to cap it all, the sun was blazing cheerfully overhead.

"After you, Monsieur le Procureur . . ."

The door opened before they had time to ring the bell. Old Elisa ushered them all in. Judge Forlacroix had retired to a remote corner of the big room. The situation was embarrassing. No one quite knew whether or not to greet him or shake him by the hand.

"You'll find the keys in all the doors, gentlemen."

Maigret noticed Lise, the Judge's daughter, sitting in an armchair, watching them with wide-eyed astonishment. A beam of light from the setting sun kindled a lock of her hair to a fiery red. Strange! He had not noticed last night that she had red, flaming red, hair.

"Be so good as to lead the way, Chief Superintendent," sighed the Public Prosecutor, very much the man of the world, deprecating the need to intrude into another man's home, and anxious to get it over as quickly as possible.

"This way . . . This is the girl's bedroom. The Judge's is at the end of the passage. . . . And this is the fruit loft. . . ."

The six men, still wearing their hats and coats, peered about them, bent down, touched some object here and there, shook their heads.

"This cupboard contains tools. This hammer here could be the murder weapon. It has been checked for fingerprints, but there are none. . . ."

"Gloves?" inquired the Public Prosecutor loftily, clearly impressed by the shrewdness of his own observation.

It was a little as if they were viewing the effects of a bankrupt, prior to an auction. Were they going to be admitted to the Judge's bedroom? Maigret opened the door. The room was of modest proportions, soberly but tastefully furnished. Everywhere, there was this combination of rustic simplicity and refinement.

Inspector Méjat was not with them. Maigret had posted him outside the house with instructions to keep watch on any loiterers, and note their reactions and comments. Right at the front was Didine, shaking her head, affronted at being relegated to the role of spectator, she who, when all was said and done, had been the prime mover in the affair.

After a whispered exchange in a corner with the Examining Magistrate, the Public Prosecutor nodded and went across to Maigret.

"I understand that it is your wish that nothing should be done about arresting him for at least the next two or three days? The situation is somewhat delicate, don't you think? Extremely delicate, in fact, since there is no doubt that the offense of concealing the body, at least, is proven. Well, if you're prepared to take the responsibility . . . It's your reputation. . . . You'll require a warrant, I suppose, in case you need to make an arrest? Perhaps you would prefer the name to be left blank?"

Satisfied that he had done his duty, he screwed up his eyes, which was his way of smiling.

"Very well, then, gentlemen . . ."

They began to disperse. The formalities were at an end. Doctor Brénéol detached himself apologetically from the rest, saying that he wished to stay on at the house with his friend Forlacroix. It only remained for the others to get into their cars. Hats were raised, handshakes exchanged.

Maigret heaved a great sigh.

At last he was free to begin his investigations!

There she was, facing him, very stiff, her lips pursed.

"When you are ready to see me, there are things I could tell you."

"But of course, Madame Didine! Let me see now . . . I'll call on you this very evening, if I may."

Drawing her shawl close about her shoulders, she stumped off. Little clumps of people were gathered here and there. Everyone was watching Maigret. A few impudent boys scampered at his heels, one of them even going so far as to mimic the Chief Superintendent's lumbering walk.

The little self-contained world was closing in on itself. The official proceedings were over, the legal dignitaries had departed, and now the village could resume its normal life, the only difference being the presence of Maigret, who had begun, as it were, to dig himself in. There was no point in turning on the children and sending them packing. They would get used to him in time.

Catching sight of the Mayor standing on the porch of his domain, Maigret went across to have a word with him.

"It occurred to me just now, Chief Superintendent . . . Obviously, you'll need somewhere to work . . . I'd be delighted to let you have the key to the town hall."

An excellent idea! The all-white council chamber had great charm, and Maigret lost no time in taking possession of it. He wanted to get the feel of it, and make himself at home there. The stove on the right. He would have to arrange for it to be lit every morning, and kept going throughout the day. He put his pipe on the table, with his tobacco pouch beside it. The window looked out onto a courtyard with a lime tree, and beyond it an iron-barred gate, which opened onto a street leading down to the sea.

Whose were those rapid footsteps? Good. It was only Méjat.

He burst in, much out of breath.

"I say, Chief . . . I think I'm on to something. . . . Marcel Airaud . . ."

"Well?"

"I listened to what people were saying, as you told me, and there's a rumor going around about Marcel. . . . Apparently, after he left you earlier, he went down to his boat. . . . It has a motor. . . . It was seen moving out into the bay in the direction of the Pont du Brault. . . . Now as far as anyone knows, he has no business there. . . . It's the wrong time of day for mussel-gathering."

There was a telephone on the table. Maigret picked up the receiver.

"Hello, mademoiselle. Do you know of anyone with a telephone near the Pont du Brault? . . . Only one house? . . . An inn? Connect me with them, will you? . . . Chief Superintendent Maigret, that's right . . . I'm at the town hall, and I shall be needing your services a good deal, I think. . . ."

He glanced up at the electric light, which emitted a dull, yellowish glow.

"See if you can get hold of a hundred-watt bulb, Méjat. Hello, is that the Auberge du Pont du Brault? I'd be very grateful if you could give me some information, madame. . . . No, this is not the brewery. . . . Did you, by any chance, happen to spot a small motorboat any time this afternoon? . . . Yes, from l'Aiguillon . . . You say it's beached just opposite the inn? . . . A bicycle? . . . Hello! Don't hang up. . . . He had a glass of wine in your bar? . . . You don't happen to know where he went? . . . In the direction of Marans? . . . Thank you, madame . . . Yes . . . If he comes back, call me immediately at the town hall at l'Aiguillon."

He ran to the door. In the gathering dusk, he had just spotted the Police Chief getting ready to leave for Luçon.

"Officer! Come in here a minute, will you? You know the Pont du Brault, I daresay. What sort of a place is it?"

"It's right at the end there, slapped in the middle of the marshes. A canal runs from the far end of the bay to Marans, which is about ten kilometers inland. It's virtually uninhabited, except for a few shacks, miles from anywhere."

"Could you arrange to have the area combed by your men? I'm looking for a man named Marcel Airaud. He's a hefty fellow, all of six feet tall, a strikingly handsome outdoor type, wearing fishermen's clothes. One could hardly fail to notice him. He left here in his boat, which is now beached somewhere near the Auberge du Pont du Brault. He left there on a borrowed bicycle."

"You don't think he . . ."

"I don't think anything at this stage, officer. . . . Can I rely on you?"

Should he call on Didine now, or wait until after dinner? He decided to go at once. Night had fallen. The grinding of winches could be heard, and the sky was lit by two intersecting lighthouse beams.

A gnarled vine covered the whole length of the wall. The door and shutters were painted green.

"Come in, Chief Superintendent. . . . I was beginning to wonder if I had done anything . . ."

A cat leaped down from a cane armchair. Hulot rose from his seat by the fire, and, out of respect, removed his long meerschaum pipe from his mouth.

"Take a seat, Chief Superintendent. . . . You will have a little glass of something? Justin, fetch the glasses from the cupboard."

She wiped them. There was an oilcloth cover on the table, and, in one corner, a very high bed, completely smothered by an enormous red eiderdown.

"The Chief Superintendent would be more comfortable in your armchair. . . . Oh, yes, I insist! With all that's been happening, I forgot to keep the fire going. . . . You'd better keep your hat on. . . ."

She chattered on, just to keep the ball rolling, but it was plain that her mind was elsewhere, and that she had not for a moment lost sight of her objective. She did not resume her seat. Her hands fluttered ceaselessly, as if she could not think what to do with them. And seeing that she was getting no help from Maigret, she felt cornered. Abruptly, she rounded on him with an apparently unpremeditated question:

"Have you found out about the child?"

So! There was a child mixed up in this business, was there?

52

"I thought so. Nobody's said a thing to you. The people around here are not much given to chatter, especially in the presence of strangers. Mind you, I'm not saying that, later on, when they're more used to you . . .

"As for me, I'm on your side, as I was just saying to Hulot. . . .

"Of course, I know you have already questioned Thérèse. I saw that for myself."

How could she have seen? Had she been spying on Maigret through a chink in the curtains? He would not put it past her. No doubt she and her husband had been keeping a close watch on every step taken by the Chief Superintendent in the course of his investigations.

"An elderly couple like ourselves, with nothing else to do, have time for reflection, you see. A little drop more? Oh, but I insist. A drop of something warming never did anyone any harm. . . . Not for you, Justin. You know it doesn't agree with you."

And she moved the bottle out of reach of her husband.

"How old would you take Thérèse to be? To look at her, you'd think she was just a child. But she must be all of twenty-three. It wouldn't surprise me to learn that she was twenty-four. . . . Well, anyway, she was barely sixteen when she began setting her cap for Marcel. Yes! I know you've talked to him, too. A fine, strapping young man like that, and a substantial property owner into the bargain, with two houses of his own, and mussel beds, and I don't know what besides, could have any girl he wanted. Whereas Thérèse is a nobody. Her mother sells oysters and mussels off a barrow to the summer visitors across the water. . . .

"All the same, she got him in the end! It was plain to everyone, about three years ago, that she was pregnant. . . .

"But even people of that sort have their pride. . . . She left

53

the village, ostensibly to get work in the town. . . . A few months later, she came back, and by then she was a lot thinner, I can tell you!

"And, what's more, I know where she goes every month, when she has her two days off. She goes to Lucon to see her child, who is being taken care of by the wife of a railway signalman.

"What do you think of that?"

To tell the truth, he had, as yet, no views on the matter. Thérèse and Marcel . . . Right! Thérèse had a hold on him.

"Mind you, this was three years ago! It wasn't until much later that Marcel took to spending his nights in the Judge's house. . . . You'll have found out about that already, I'm sure. . . . And there were others before him. And after him, too, I shouldn't wonder. . . . But do you know what I think? I think he's different from the rest. . . . The others were just taking advantage, if you see what I mean. You know what men are like."

She shot a sly, indulgent glance at her customs officer, who, with his squint more pronounced than ever, assumed an air of great innocence.

"But it was different for Marcel. He was in love with her— I'm sure of it—and I bet you anything you like he would have been ready to marry her, even though she's not quite right in the head. . . .

"Now, supposing there was someone in Lucon known to Thérèse, and that she'd asked him to come here and avenge the wrong done to her . . . Anyone could get into the Judge's house. It's about as secure as a barn. . . . Look over there. . . . Daylight's going, but you can still see the white expanse of the terrace. It's an easy climb for any man. All he'd have to do would be to scramble over the balustrade and sneak into the house through the fruit loft. . . . The window is kept open

54

most of the time.... Locking the girl in her bedroom is as much use as trying to keep water in a sieve...."

Maigret gave a start, becoming aware, suddenly, of his own train of thought. For several seconds now, he had been only half listening to the droning of the old woman's voice, and meanwhile, very gradually, an absurd idea had begun to take shape in his mind. It was merely the ghost of an idea so far, but if he were to let it be, might it not take on some substance?

"The Judge's house is about as secure as a ..."

In his mind's eye, he saw Didine sitting in his office in Lucon; he heard her clear, sharp voice describing, with quite terrifying precision, a series of dramatic events, events which, however, she personally had not witnessed!

Her irrefutable logic ... Her meticulous calculations of the tides ... An experienced police detective could scarcely have done better.... And the pair of them on guard outside the house, one at the back, the other at the front ... And spying out the land through binoculars, into the bargain!

It was altogether too far-fetched. He had only to look around this poorly furnished peasant dwelling, with its high bed and mountainous eiderdown, its thick drinking glasses on the oilcloth-covered table, and Didine's white kerchief, to banish all such thoughts from his mind.

"By the way, did you know the Judge at all before he came to live here?"

He had struck home. He was certain of it. She gave an almost imperceptible start. He noted the very slight tensing of her muscles.

"It depends what you mean by that.... I knew him when I was a very little girl.... I was born in the house just opposite the town hall. The Judge used to come and stay with his cousin during the holidays.... When his cousin died, he inherited the house...."

"Did he go on coming after he was married?"

"Not every year," she replied, suddenly on her guard.

"Did you know his wife?"

"I saw her around, like everyone else. She was a fine-looking woman."

"If I'm not mistaken, you would be about the same age as Forlacroix?"

"I believe he's a year older than I am."

"You went to live with your husband in Concarneau, and he settled in Versailles. . . . When you came back to l'Aiguillon, he had already returned as a widower, to live in the house next door."

"He's not a widower," she retorted.

Maigret sprang to his feet with such force that the cane armchair creaked ominously.

"His wife left him, but she's still alive."

"Are you sure?"

"I'm sure she was a month ago, at any rate, considering I saw her as plainly as I see you. . . . She got out of a car, and rang his bell. . . . They stood talking for a few minutes in the hall, and then she left."

It would not have surprised him if she had gone on to tell him the number of the car's license. But maybe that was asking too much.

"You have only yourself to blame for not having learned all this before now. Instead of chasing about all over the place, keeping out of my way, and ignoring my poor husband . . . I may as well tell you now . . . he was beginning to get thoroughly discouraged. . . . Isn't that so, Justin? You needn't be afraid to speak your mind to the Chief Superintendent. He knows what free speech is all about, and there's no reason for anyone to keep silent if he has nothing to hide. Drink up, Chief Superintendent. . . . What else do you want to know?

56

I haven't finished, by any means. I could go on like this all night. . . . But I need time. I can't remember everything all at once."

She had said enough. More than enough, in fact! She was a devilishly cunning old crone.

"Take the doctor, for instance. . . . It may or may not interest you, but he's the Judge's closest friend. . . . Have you seen his wife? She's a big woman, dark, and heavily made up. She's always very showily dressed. She has a daughter of the first bed, as they say hereabouts. Wait till you see her. She's nothing much to look at. But that doesn't alter the fact that Doctor Brénéol is crazy about her. He's always taking her out in his car without his wife. They travel as far away from here as they can get. And someone from the village, who shall be nameless for the present, saw them coming out of a hotel in La Rochelle. . . ."

Maigret felt exhausted, as if he had just returned from a long walk.

"I'll come and see you again soon, I promise. Thanks for your help."

Henceforth, apparently, as far as she was concerned, they were fellow conspirators, for in this spirit she held out her hand to him, and signed to her husband to do likewise.

"Feel free to come whenever you like. . . . And you may rest assured that you'll get nothing but the truth from me."

There was a light in one window of the Judge's house, the window of Lise's bedroom. Had she already gone to bed? Maigret made a tour of the garden. By this time, the charwomen must have gone home. Which left just the two of them alone together in the house.

He was already beginning to feel at home in the bar of the Hôtel du Port. As he went in, he was struck by the way Thérèse looked at him. It was only natural that she should be feeling anxious, but was she not also hoping to read in his face signs of any possible new developments?

Méjat, leaning on the bar counter, was sipping an apéritif in the company of the landlord.

"Tell me, Thérèse, do you know of any reason why Marcel should have gone to Marans?"

"Marans?" she repeated warily, very much on her guard, and determined to give nothing away.

"Since you are such old friends, I thought he might have said something to you."

"He doesn't have to account to me for his movements."

"What's for dinner?"

"Soup, plaice, and, if you would care for one, a pork chop with cabbage."

"Come and join me, Méjat!"

Méjat had news for him. A photograph of the victim had been shown to the staff of every hotel in Lucon, but the victim had not spent the night at any one of them. There was nothing to do but wait. The newspapers surely . . .

"Don't you feel sleepy, Chief?"

"I intend to go to bed right after dinner, and I won't get up before eight tomorrow morning."

He was hungry. He allowed his mind to wander as he watched Thérèse going to and fro. She was a very ordinary, rather unhealthy-looking girl. A little hotel chambermaid, whom one would scarcely notice in normal circumstances, in her black dress, black stockings, and white apron. The room was empty. All the men were at home eating their fish soup, and would not gather again at the bar until after dinner.

The telephone rang. The instrument was fixed to the wall under the stairs. Thérèse went to answer it.

"Hello . . . Yes . . . What are you . . .?"

"Is it for me?" asked Maigret.

She was listening intently.

"Yes . . . Yes . . . I don't know. . . . I haven't heard. . . ."

"What is it?" called out the landlord from the kitchen.

She hung up abruptly.

"Nothing . . . It was for me."

Maigret had already snatched up the receiver.

"Hello, mademoiselle. Chief Superintendent Maigret speaking. You put a call through to this number just now. Could you tell me where the caller was speaking from? . . . What's that? . . . Marans? . . . Yes, find out the number for me, and call me back."

He returned to the table. Thérèse, looking deathly pale, served him without a word. Presently the telephone rang again.

"From a café? . . . The Café Arthur? . . . Get me the police station at Marans, mademoiselle. . . . Hello. Is that the duty sergeant? . . . Chief Superintendent Maigret here . . . I want you to go to the Café Arthur. . . . You know it? . . . That's good. . . . A man has just telephoned from there. . . . Name is Marcel Airaud. . . . Take him to the police station, and let me know as soon as you've got him."

An oppressive silence. The chops. The cabbage. Thérèse scuttling to and fro, with eyes averted.

At the end of half an hour, the shrilling of the telephone bell.

"Hello! . . . Yes? . . . Oh! . . . No . . . Wait for further instructions. . . . That's right."

Time went by. Thérèse still could not bring herself to look at the hunched figure of Maigret, standing under the stairs with his back toward the room. Stealthily, the Chief Superintendent pressed down the receiver rest, to cut off the caller, but he went on talking as if he had not done so.

"Is he hurt? . . . Just the same, you'd better take him to the jail in Lucon. . . . Thanks . . . Good night, Sergeant."

He returned broodingly to his seat, sighed, considered whether or not to have some cheese, then, taking advantage of Thérèse's temporary absence in the kitchen, he winked at Méjat, and whispered:

"Damn the man! No sooner had he made his phone call then he disappeared. . . . I wonder what he could possibly have had to say to her."

5

The Confession

•

Had he really acted cruelly? Thérèse detested him, that went without saying. Every now and then, she would give such a black look that Maigret could not help smiling. This so confused the poor little thing that she could not make up her mind whether to spring at him and scratch his face or smile back at him.

For over an hour he played her like a fish at the end of a line. However she might come and go, running to and fro at the beck and call of the customers, pausing only to pick at some food on the edge of the kitchen table, she could not escape Maigret's impassive scrutiny. Perhaps, in the long run, she even found it reassuring. After all, was it not possible that this big stolid man, absently puffing at his pipe, was more her friend than her enemy?

She swung back and forth from one extreme to the other, from intense agitation and anger to something akin to friendliness. By way of overture, she asked him, after she had cleared the table, what he would like to drink.

But no sooner had she brought him his glass of Calvados than she felt impelled to hasten from the room. When she returned, her eyes were red, and her nose running.

61

There was a party of men playing cards and, while serving their drinks, she broke a glass. Later, she rose from the kitchen table, having barely touched her evening meal.

At last she could stand it no longer, and she spoke to the proprietress. Maigret could not hear what was said, but could guess from their gestures. Thérèse, drooping as befitted one who was feeling unwell, gazed up at the ceiling. The proprietress responded with a shrug.

"Very well, dear, you may go."

Thérèse took off her apron, returned to the bar to check that everything had been cleared away, and looked imploringly at Maigret.

"Before you go to bed, Méjat, I want you to make sure that the Judge's house is still under surveillance, back and front, and that there is also another policeman on guard outside young Forlacroix's place."

He got up and started upstairs. The stairway was so narrow that he was almost wedged between the wall and the banister. All this part of the building was new. The woodwork was too light, and the walls crudely whitewashed, and some of the white rubbed off on his clothes.

Maigret went into his room, leaving the door open. A few minutes passed, at the end of which, somewhat surprised, indeed almost disappointed, he glanced out into the corridor. Then he smiled.

It would be at least an hour or two before the others came up to bed. What if Méjat did find the Chief Superintendent in the chambermaid's bedroom? No doubt he would have his own cockeyed notions about that. Well, all the worse for him. He went in. She was standing there waiting for him. She had let down her hair, which was usually pinned up in a bun at the nape of her neck. Framed in a dark cloud of hair, her features seemed more finely drawn, her nose sharper, her expression more reserved.

62

Seated on the edge of the iron bedstead, Maigret observed her at his leisure, and it was she who was obliged to take the initiative.

"You're making a big mistake in picking on Marcel. I know him better than anyone, and . . ."

She was striving after the right effect, like an actress, but failing to achieve it.

"We were planning to get married this summer. Doesn't that prove . . . ?"

"Because of the child?"

She showed no surprise.

"Because of the child, and other things. We love each other. . . . There's nothing strange about that, is there?"

"What is rather strange is that you should have waited until the child was three years old to regularize the situation. . . . Look at me, Thérèse. You can take my word for it that you have nothing to gain by lying. . . . What did Marcel say to you on the telephone?"

She gave him a long look, and then sighed.

"Oh, well. I may live to regret this, but it can't be helped. . . . He wanted to know if any papers were found in the pockets . . ."

"Whose pockets?"

"The dead man's, I suppose."

"And you said no?"

"I imagine that if anything of any importance had been found, I would have heard about it. . . . But just because Marcel asked me that, it doesn't mean he killed him. . . . I repeat, we were planning to get married."

"That doesn't alter the fact that he spent most of his nights in Lise Forlacroix's bedroom."

"He doesn't love her!"

"He has an odd way of showing it."

"You know what men are like. . . . It had nothing to do

63

with love. . . . He told me so, often. . . . It was an obsession with him, and he swore to me that he would get over it in time."

"That's not true."

She gave a start, then her expression hardened, and she began berating him with coarse vigor.

"Who are you to say what is or is not true? Were you there to see what went on? You'll be telling me next that it's not true that I once saw him leave the Judge's house, not by the window, but by the front door. And that the Judge wasn't all over him, and that he didn't know every single thing that was going on. . . . Who comes out of this business worse, I'd like to know? I don't deny that I gave birth to a child, but I've never been one to lure men into my bedroom. . . ."

"Just a minute! When was it that you saw Marcel and the Judge together?"

"About a month ago . . . Let me think . . . It was shortly before Christmas."

"And you say that you had the impression that they were on friendly terms? What did Marcel say when you asked him for an explanation?"

She was going to lie again. He could tell by the way the tip of her nose was quivering.

"He told me I had nothing to worry about. Everything was going to be all right. In four or five months' time we would be married, and we would set up house across the water, somewhere near Charron, and we would never see those people again. . . . He loves me, d'you hear? He had no earthly reason to kill a man he had never even set eyes on. . . ."

Footsteps on the stairs, in the corridor. The opening and shutting of a door. Méjat was back. He whistled to himself as he got ready for bed.

"Is there nothing more you want to tell me, Thérèse, my

64

dear? Think hard. So far everything you have told me has been a mixture of truth and lies, and the lies make it difficult for me to take account of those parts of your story that are true."

He stood up. He was too tall and too broad for the room. Suddenly, when he was least expecting it, Thérèse threw herself into his arms and burst into frantic sobs.

"There, there," he murmured, as if to a child. "That will do, now. Tell me all about it."

She was sobbing so loudly that Méjat, whose room was just across the passage, opened his door.

"Calm down, my dear. You don't want the whole house to hear you. . . . You don't feel like talking now, is that it?"

She nodded, and once more buried her face in Maigret's chest.

"You're making a big mistake. . . . Well, never mind. You'd better go to bed. . . . Would you like me to give you something to help you sleep?"

Still behaving like a distraught child, she nodded. He produced a soluble sleeping tablet, dropped it in a glass and ran a little water over it.

"You'll feel better in the morning."

She looked up at him, her eyes brimming with tears, and her cheeks wet. As she drank from the glass, he took the opportunity of backing hastily out of the room.

"Phew!" he sighed, as he stretched out at long last on his bed, in which he felt almost as cramped as in Thérèse's little room.

He awoke the following morning to frost and sunshine. Thérèse served him his breakfast, looking more resentful than ever. The barber in l'Aiguillon apparently stocked Méjat's brand of brilliantine, for he stank of it to high heaven.

Maigret pottered about the village with his hands in his pockets. He watched the mussel-gatherers returning, the baskets of mussels, the sea, greenish-blue in the distance, the bridge, which he had never yet traversed to the end, beyond which lay a small branch-line station and a few modestly priced houses scattered among the pines.

A policeman paced up and down outside the Judge's house. The wooden shutters were open. Maigret was beginning to feel at home in this colorful little world. Several people wished him good day, though there were others who merely stared balefully at him. The Mayor, who was loading mussels on a truck, called out to him:

"There are several telegrams for you. I've left them on your table at the town hall. The Chief of Police is waiting there to see you, I believe."

It was late. Maigret had overslept. Unhurriedly, he made his way to his office, just as he used to do in the old days, by way of the Saint-Antoine district and the Ile Saint-Louis, when things were slack at the Quai des Orfèvres.

There stood the plaster bust of the Republic in its appointed place. Fire was crackling in the stove. An unopened bottle of white wine and some glasses stood on his desk, by courtesy of the Mayor, no doubt.

The Chief of Police followed Maigret into the room. The latter, having taken off his hat and coat, was about to ask a question when his attention was diverted by a veritable explosion of children's voices. It was a pleasant sound, like listening to a fireworks display. There, under his very windows, the entire school had debouched, to enjoy the midmorning recess in the sun. The playground was dotted with frozen puddles, and the dull clunk of wooden clogs could be heard as the children slid across them. All were well wrapped up, in duffle coats or shawls, with red, blue, or green scarves around their necks.

66

"I'm listening, officer. What news of Marcel Airaud?"

"We haven't managed to find him yet, what with the flood tide, and the shacks being so widely scattered. At this time of year, many of the footpaths are almost impassable, and some of the shacks are so isolated that they can only be reached by boat."

"How are things at the Judge's house?"

"Dead quiet. No one has entered or left the house, except the two charwomen, who turned up as usual this morning."

"What about Albert Forlacroix?"

"He went out this morning, as usual, to gather mussels. One of my men has had his eye on him the whole time. . . . I thought it advisable, particularly because he is known to have a violent temper, and is inclined to flare up at the slightest provocation."

Was it sheer self-indulgence that prompted him to stand warming himself, with his back to the fire, lighting his pipe at his leisure, while there were newly arrived telegrams still unopened on the table? Or was it not, rather, that he was overscrupulous in his determination to deal with one thing at a time, to clean up his unfinished business in l'Aiguillon before turning his attention to what might be happening elsewhere?

Ironically enough, the first telegram he opened was from Madame Maigret.

HAVE DISPATCHED SUITCASE WITH CHANGE OF CLOTHING ON BUS STOP AWAITING FURTHER NEWS STOP LOVE.

"What time does the bus get here?"

"In a few minutes."

"There'll be a suitcase for me on it. I'd be much obliged if you could arrange to have it collected and delivered to the Hôtel du Port."

The next telegram, a longer one, was from Nantes.

TO CHIEF SUPERINTENDENT MAIGRET FROM THE FLYING SQUAD NANTES STOP CORPSE IDENTIFIED AS DOCTOR JANIN

67

THIRTY-FIVE YEARS OF AGE ADDRESS RUE DES EGLISES NANTES STOP LEFT HOME TUESDAY 11TH JANUARY WITHOUT LUGGAGE STOP INQUIRIES CONTINUING STOP TELEPHONE IF FURTHER DETAILS REQUIRED.

The Chief of Police had just come back into the room. Maigret handed him the telegram, remarking with apparent indifference:

"He was younger than he looked."

Then he turned the handle of the telephone, bade the switchboard girl an affable good morning, and asked her to connect him with the Flying Squad headquarters in Nantes.

He was enjoying all this, though it was pure routine. Well, on to the next thing.

The third telegram was from Versailles, in reply to one sent by him.

WHEN LAST HEARD OF MADAME FORLACROIX NÉE VALENTINE CONSTANTINESCO RESIDING AT VILLA DES ROCHES-GRISES RUE COMMANDANT-MARCHAND NICE.

"Hello! Is that Flying Squad headquarters, Nantes? Maigret speaking. . . . Put him on. . . . Guillaume? . . . Of course, my dear fellow . . . I'm fine . . . You haven't wasted much time. . . . Yes, I'm listening. . . ."

It was not Maigret's habit to take notes. If he had a pencil in his hand and a sheet of paper in front of him, it was merely in order to doodle meaningless squibbles, quite unconnected with the case.

"Emile Janin . . . Medical School, Montpelier University . . . Of humble origin, born in Roussillon . . . Two years as a resident at Saint Anne's Hospital . . . That's interesting. . . . It means he must have had considerable experience with psychiatric cases. . . . Well! Well! A bit of a loner, would you say? . . . Signed on as a ship's doctor . . . What ship? . . . the *Vengeur* . . . the *Vengeur* sailed on a world cruise three or four years back. . . . That explains the clothes bought in Panama. . . . Reports not very favorable . . . Too independent by half . . . Returned to civilian life, and settled in Nantes, where he set up in practice as a psychoanalyst . . .

"Hello, mademoiselle . . . May I trouble you to get me another number? The Sûreté in Nice, Alpes-Maritimes . . . It's very urgent. . . . Thanks . . . Of course, I know you're doing your best, and to show I appreciate it, I'll call on you with a box of chocolates before I leave. . . . You prefer *marrons glacées?* I'll make a note of it."

And turning to the Chief of Police:

"I have a feeling that I may be making an arrest before very long."

Intuition? No sooner were the words out of his mouth than the telephone began ringing insistently. The children had returned to their classrooms. Naturally, it was not yet his call to Nice.

"Chief Superintendent Maigret? One moment, please . . . Monsieur Bourdeille-Jaminet, the Public Prosecutor, wishes to speak to you."

The voice sounded distant, magisterial, remote from the common concerns of daily life.

"You have been informed of the identity of the dead man, have you not? I was wondering whether, in the circumstances . . . I took a grave risk in agreeing . . . I take it you still have the warrant? . . . Well, the fact is, Chief Superintendent, that, having consulted with the Examining Magistrate, I have come to the conclusion that the wise course would be to . . . ."

Méjat had come into the room, and was sitting discreetly in a corner, casting sidelong glances at the tempting bottle of white wine.

"I have Nice on the line for you."

"Thanks. Is that the Sûreté Nationale?"

Succinctly, he issued his instructions, and when he was finished, he glanced down mechanically at the sheet of paper on his desk, and saw that what he had drawn was the outline of a fleshy mouth, a pair of sensual pouting lips, such as are to be seen in the paintings of Renoir.

He tore the sheet into little shreds and threw them into the fire.

"I think . . ." he began.

Someone was crossing the courtyard. It was the daughter of old Elisa, who, with her mother, worked for the Judge.

"Bring her in, Méjat."

"I have a letter for Monsieur Maigret."

He took it, dismissed the girl, and slowly tore open the envelope.

What now? It was the first time he had seen the Judge's handwriting, a fine, neat, cramped script, perhaps a little too self-consciously refined. The lines were perfectly straight and evenly spaced. The paper, though by no means showy, was handmade and of the finest quality.

Chief Superintendent,

Forgive me for writing to you instead of calling upon you either in your office in the town hall or at your hotel. But, as you are aware, I am very reluctant to leave my daughter unattended.

I have been thinking a great deal since our last meeting, and have at least concluded that the time has come for me to reveal certain facts.

I am perfectly willing to call upon you whenever and wherever you wish, though I confess that, even though it may be somewhat irregular, I should prefer it if you would do me the honor of paying me another visit.

I need not remind you that I am always at home, and that any time convenient to you would suit me.

Thanking you in advance for your kind consideration, I re-

70

main, Chief Superintendent, your most humble and obedient servant.

Maigret stuffed the letter into his pocket without offering to show it either to the Chief of Police or to Méjat, though both were patently dying of curiosity.

"Have the newspapers arrived yet?" he asked.

"They must be being delivered now. They come in on the mail truck, and I saw it go past while you were on the telephone."

"Would you go and get me one, Méjat? And at the same time, you might check that, apart from the charwomen, no one has been to see the Judge this morning."

He seemed less cheerful than he had been earlier. He wore a brooding expression. He prowled restlessly about the room, changing the position of things. Then his gaze rested thoughtfully on the telephone and, after a moment or two, he turned the handle.

"It's I again, mademoiselle. . . . I can see it's going to have to be a very large box of *marrons glacés*. . . . Have you finished sorting the mail yet? . . . Has it gone out? . . . Any letters for Judge Forlacroix? . . . Tell me this, has he made or received any telephone calls today? . . . No? . . . Have there been any telegrams for him? . . . Thanks . . . Yes, I'm expecting another priority call, from Nice."

Méjat returned, with three other men, whom he left outside in the courtyard.

"Reporters."

"So I see."

"One from Luçon, and two from Nantes. I've brought you all the local papers."

All featured a photograph of the dead man, but there was no reference to the fact that his identity was known, and for a very good reason.

"What shall I tell them?"

"Nothing."

"They'll be livid. You won't be able to avoid them at lunch, because they're staying at the Hôtel du Port."

Maigret shrugged, and stoked the stove. Then, noticing that the children were already coming out of school, he glanced at his watch. What did those wretched fellows in Nice think they were doing, with that sun of theirs, like a tinsel disk?

He was troubled by one small, niggling point for which he could find no explanation. Why should the Judge have chosen to write that letter at that precise moment, when the corpse had just been identified? Did he know? And if he did, how could he possibly have found out?

The telephone . . . But it was still not Nice. It was Marans, to tell him that Marcel Airaud had not been traced, and that the search had been widened to take in the whole area of marshland.

Thank heaven, Nice at last! Three voices on the line at once . . .

"Clear the line, you there at Marans. . . . Oh, do hang up, for God's sake! Hello, Nice? . . . Yes, Maigret here . . . The lady in question has not set foot outside Nice for the past three weeks, you say? . . . Are you sure? . . . And she's received no telegram, either last night or this morning? . . . What? . . . I didn't quite catch that name. . . . Luchet . . . Van Uchet . . . Would you spell it, please. . . . V for Victor . . . Van Usschen . . . Yes, I'm listening. . . . A Dutchman . . . In cocoa . . . Yes! . . . I want all the information you can get. . . . If I'm not here, you can leave the message with my assistant."

Half under his breath, as if talking to himself rather than anyone else, he murmured:

"The Judge's wife has been living for years in Nice with a wealthy Dutchman by the name of Horace Van Usschen, who made his fortune in cocoa. . . ."

Then he uncorked the bottle of white wine and tossed off one glass, and then another. Presently, looking through rather than at him, he said to Méjat:

"You stay put here until I get back."

The three reporters were close on his heels, but he stubbornly ignored them. The Hôtel du Port was full. Many of the men who had gathered there for a drink before lunch came out onto the porch, curious to see where he was going. He greeted the policeman on duty outside the Judge's house with a little wave of the hand, and rang the bell.

Elisa opened the door to him.

"This way. His Honor is expecting you."

And here he was again in this spacious room, so cozy and so peaceful. Maigret noted that the Judge was ceaselessly clenching and unclenching his hands, one over the other, and that they were drained of blood.

"Do please sit down, Chief Superintendent. But first, allow me to relieve you of your coat. What I have to say may take some time and, as you see, it's very warm in here. I won't venture to offer you a glass of port, since you would doubtless feel obliged to refuse."

There was a hint of bitterness in his voice.

"Not at all."

"But, after you've heard me out, you may well feel that I am not a man with whom you would wish to be on such convivial terms."

Maigret sat down in the same armchair he had occupied the previous night, stretched out his legs, and filled his pipe.

"Do you know a man by the name of Doctor Janin?"

The Judge reflected for a moment. The name genuinely meant nothing to him.

"Janin? . . . Let me think. . . . No . . . I'm sure I don't."

"He's the man you wanted to dump in the sea."

73

An odd little gesture, signifying:

That has nothing to do with the matter in hand. It's of no importance.

He poured two glasses of port.

"Well, here's to your health!" he said. "You can't say I haven't warned you. . . . But first, I would like to ask you a question. . . ."

He was looking grave. His face, under his long, rumpled silver locks, like those of a woman, grew animated.

"In the event that I should be prevented for a time from taking care of my daughter, would you be willing to promise me, man to man, that no harm would come to her?"

"I imagine that, in such an eventuality as you envisage, the custody of your daughter would pass to your wife?"

"You will see shortly that there is no question of her being handed over to her mother. . . . Therefore . . ."

"Provided that it is within the law, I will personally see to it that she receives the best possible care."

"Thank you."

Slowly he drained his glass of port, and went to a drawer and got out cigarettes.

"You smoke a pipe, don't you? Please feel free."

Presently, having lit a cigarette, he murmured, as he exhaled the first puff of smoke:

"That being the case, I have come to the conclusion, after giving much careful thought to the matter, that it would be the best thing all around for me to serve a term in prison."

It came as a shock. As the Judge was speaking, a trill of notes could be heard coming from the piano above their heads. The Judge looked up at the ceiling. When he spoke again, his voice was hoarse with emotion, as if suppressed sobs were rising in his throat.

"I killed a man, Chief Superintendent."

Outside, the policeman's hobnailed boots could be heard ringing on the hard paving stones.

"And now that I've said it, do you still feel like finishing your port?"

He took an old gold watch from his pocket, and pressed the catch to open the cover.

"It's twelve o'clock. . . . It makes no difference to me, of course, but you may prefer to take a break for lunch. It would hardly be proper for me to invite you to eat at my table."

He poured himself another drink, and then went across and sat down, facing Maigret, on the other side of the crackling fire.

6

The Two Englishwomen of Versailles

•

About one o'clock, the policeman on duty outside the Judge's house began showing signs of anxiety, and every time he went past the windows he moved a little closer, hoping to make out what was happening inside.

At half past one, he went right up to the window and pressed his face against the glass. It took him a second or two to register the two figures seated in armchairs on either side of the fireplace, their heads mysteriously wreathed in clouds of smoke.

It was at about this time that a tinkle of cutlery and a murmur of female voices could be heard in a room nearby. Lise Forlacroix, Maigret presumed, was having her lunch.

From time to time, he crossed his legs and, a little later, uncrossed them, to tap out his pipe on the heel of his shoe. The tiles of the hearth were already thick with ash. But what did it matter now? The Judge, from force of habit, extinguished his cigarettes in a green china ashtray, and the growing pile of little white-and-brown stubs spoke volumes.

The quiet murmur of their voices continued. Every now and then, Maigret would ask a question, or raise an objection. Forlacroix would reply crisply and precisely, just as he wrote.

At a quarter past two, the telephone rang. They both started at the sound, as if they had forgotten the existence of the outside world. Forlacroix looked inquiringly at Maigret. Should he answer it? Maigret nodded.

"Hello . . . Yes . . . I'll put him on. . . . It's for you, Chief Superintendent."

"Hello, Chief . . . Sorry to disturb you . . . Maybe I was wrong, but I was beginning to get worried. . . . There's nothing the matter, I hope. . . ."

The Judge returned to his seat and fidgeted with his hands as he gazed into the log fire.

"I want you to hire a car for me. . . . Yes, now, at once . . . See that it's here within the next half hour. . . . No! Nothing special . . ."

And he, too, resumed his seat.

When the taxi arrived at the door, bringing Méjat with it, the Chief Superintendent was alone in the big room, pacing up and down eating a pâté sandwich. On the table was a nearly empty bottle of vintage Burgundy. The air was so thick with smoke that it was almost impossible to breathe.

Méjat stared wide-eyed at the Chief Superintendent, looking totally thunderstruck.

"Is it over? Are you going to arrest him? Am I to come with you?"

"You're to stay here."

"What do you want me to do?"

"Get out your notebook. Write this down. . . . Thérèse, the girl from the hotel . . . the two Hulots, Didine and the customs man . . . Albert Forlacroix . . . and, most important of all, Marcel Airaud, who must be found at all costs."

"And you want me to keep a watch on the others you mentioned?"

Footsteps on the stairs.

"You can go now."

77

Reluctantly, Méjat went. The Judge appeared, wearing his coat and hat, looking very dapper, very much the gentleman.

"Do you mind if I telephone Doctor Brénéol to ask him about the nursing home?"

Lise Forlacroix was upstairs with the two charwomen. They could hear her moving about.

"Is that you, Brénéol? . . . No, nothing to worry about . . . I just wanted to ask you if you happened to know of a good nursing home anywhere around La Roche-sur-Yon. . . . Yes . . . Villa Albert Premier . . . Just before you get to the town? . . . Thanks . . . Good-bye . . ."

Old Elisa was the first to come downstairs, carrying two suitcases, which she took out to the car. Next came her daughter with the hand luggage. Lise was the last to appear. She was almost lost in the folds of a soft fur coat with the collar turned up.

It all happened very quickly. Lise and her father got in the back. Maigret sat next to the driver. Didine watched from the corner of the street. Passers-by stopped in their tracks. They had to drive the whole length of the main street, past the hotel, past the post office and the town hall. Curtains twitched. A bunch of children started running, trying to keep up with the car.

In the rearview mirror, Maigret could see Lise and her father. As far as he could tell, the Judge never once let go of his daughter's hand throughout the journey. Night was closing in as they approached La Roche-sur-Yon. They had to stop several times to ask the way to the Villa Albert Premier. There was some delay before they were received by the Superintendent and shown the rooms. Everything was white, too white, like the clothes of the doctor and the nurses.

"Room number seven . . . Very well."

There were five of them in the room, Lise, a nurse, Maigret, the Judge, and the Superintendent.

Only three went out into the corridor. Lise and the nurse remained behind on the other side of the door. Lise had not shed a tear. Father and daughter had not exchanged a parting kiss.

"In about an hour's time, a police inspector will be arriving to stand guard outside this door."

A few more miles, and they were in the town. The prison gate. The few formalities of committal. No doubt by sheer chance, Maigret and the Judge had no time to take leave of one another.

A brasserie. A fat cashier. A railway timetable. A well-chilled glass of beer.

"Could you bring me some writing paper and a ham sandwich . . . Oh, and another beer!"

He wrote out his official report for the Public Prosecutor, drafted several telegrams, and caught his train with only seconds to spare. Then he had to hang about at the Gare de Saint-Pierre from midnight till two in the morning.

The Gare d'Orsay . . . At eight o'clock in the morning, shaved and refreshed, he emerged from his apartment on Boulevard Richard-Lenoir. The sun was rising over Paris. He changed buses at the stop nearest to Police Headquarters, and from there he could see the windows of the office that had once been his.

The January weather, sunny but with a nip in the air, persisted as he got off the train at Versailles and sauntered in leisurely fashion, with his pipe clenched between his teeth, down Avenue de Paris. By now it was nine o'clock. And it was at this point that he suddenly felt as if his personality had been split in two, as if he were living on two separate planes simultaneously. Oh, he was still Chief Superintendent Maigret all right, Maigret who had been packed off to Luçon in disgrace. His hands were in the pockets of Maigret's overcoat, and he was smoking Maigret's pipe.

All around him was the real Versailles, Versailles as it was now, and not as it had been at any given moment in the past.

It was very quiet on the avenue, especially at the far end, where massive portals and high walls hid the prettiest little private houses in all the world.

And yet it all seemed somehow a little unreal, like location shots in a film, a travel documentary perhaps . . . A succession of images projected on a screen . . . And at the same time, the voice of a man setting the scene, the voice of a commentator.

The voice, thin and colorless, was that of Judge Forlacroix, and inevitably it evoked, superimposed on the buildings of Versailles, the big room at l'Aiguillon, the crackling logs, the tiled hearth littered with pipe ash, the cigarette butts in the green china ashtray.

"My family settled in Versailles three generations back. My father, who was an attorney, lived the whole of his life in a house on Avenue de Paris, which had belonged to his father before him. . . . A white wall . . . A spacious gateway flanked by stone pillars . . . A gilded escutcheon and . . . Our name engraved on a brass plate . . ."

And there it was. Maigret had reached the house, but the escutcheon was gone, and so was the brass plate. The door was open. A footman in striped waistcoat was beating carpets on the pavement.

"Through the gateway into a small courtyard paved with those same little round stone tiles as are found in the great court of the Palace of Versailles and which are known as the king's tiles . . . Grass sprouting between the paving stones . . . A porch with a glass roof . . . Tall windows with small panes . . . Everything bathed in light . . . A hall with a bronze foun-

tain in the center, and beyond, a formal garden in the style of the Trianon . . . With its lawns and roses . . . I was born there, like my father before me. . . . For years I lived there, devoting myself to the pursuit of the arts and literature, and the enjoyment of good food and good wine. . . . I became a justice of the peace, and had no ambition to rise any further. . . ."

Was it not perhaps easier to understand all this here in Versailles than in the seclusion of l'Aiguillon?

"A small circle of close friends . . . Holidays in Italy and Greece . . . An adequate income . . . A few good pieces of furniture, and a decent library . . . When my father died, I was thirty-five years old, and still a bachelor. . . ."

No doubt there were people very like Forlacroix still residing in these houses, wholly wrapped up in the pursuit of gracious living.

The footman was beginning to look suspiciously at this man in the heavy overcoat who was gazing so intently at the home of his employers.

But Maigret had a call to make, and it was surely too early for that.

Slowly, he walked back up the avenue, took a turning to the right, then to the left, pausing to read the street names, and finally reached a four-story house, somewhat larger than the rest, whose rooms were doubtless rented to innumerable tenants.

"Does Mademoiselle Dochet still live here?" he inquired of the concierge.

"One moment! There she is, on her way upstairs with her shopping."

He caught up with her on the second floor, just as she was turning the brass knob of her apartment door. She looked almost as old as the house.

"Excuse me, mademoiselle. You are the owner of this building, are you not? I'm making inquiries about someone who used to live here. . . . All of twenty-five years ago, it must be . . ."

She was seventy.

"Please come in. . . . Excuse me a moment, while I turn off the gas in the kitchen, or my milk will boil over. . . ."

Latticed windowpanes . . . Crimson carpets . . .

"The man in question was a musician, famous as a virtuoso in his day. His name was Constantinesco."

"I remember him! He lived in the apartment above."

So it was true. And once again he seemed to hear the Judge's voice providing a running commentary:

"He was a bohemian, and I fancy he had the makings of a genius. He made quite a name for himself at the outset of his career. He gave recitals almost everywhere you can think of, including America. Somewhere on his travels he acquired a wife, and fathered a daughter. I don't know what became of the wife, but he kept the daughter with him. . . . Finally, he landed in a tumble-down apartment in Versailles, where he earned a meager living by giving violin lessons. My friends and I used to amuse ourselves by playing chamber music, and one evening, when we were short of a violinist, someone brought him along to my house."

A faint flush had colored the Judge's cheeks as he looked at his white hands and murmured:

"I play the piano a little."

As for the old spinster, her comment was:

"He was half off his head. He used to fly into the most frightful rages. I could hear him thundering down the stairs, shouting his head off. . . ."

"What about the daughter?"

The landlady pursed her lips.

"Now that she's married, and done very well for herself,

from what I hear! ... Her husband is a magistrate, isn't he? Some people have all the luck, and they're not always the ones who most ..."

Who most what? Maigret would never know, because she refused to say another word.

There was nothing more to be learned here. He knew all there was to know. The Judge was incapable of lying.

Valentine Constantinesco ... A girl of eighteen, with a figure already well developed, and huge eyes, who set out for Paris every morning carrying her sheet music, to study at the Conservatory. She was learning the piano, and, at the same time, taking violin lessons from her father.

And thus it was that a little judge, a bachelor and an epicurean, took to spying on her from the corner of the street, and following her at a distance, and traveling on the same electric train.

Avenue de Paris ... There now! The footman had gone inside, shutting the front door behind him, that same front door which had opened for Valentine wearing her white wedding dress. . . .

A few marvelous years ... The birth of a son, then of a daughter ... Occasionally, during the summer, they and the children would spend a few weeks in the old family home at l'Aiguillon. . . .

"Take it from me, Chief Superintendent, I am not unfamiliar with the ways of the world. . . . I am not one to be blinded by happiness. . . . I often used to catch myself looking at her uneasily. . . . But when you see those eyes of hers, which will not have changed, you will understand. . . . Such innocent, unclouded eyes ... And that melodious voice ... And those dresses she wore, aquamarine and pale blue, such delicate, restrained colors, making her look like a pastel drawing ...

"I dared not admit my astonishment at having fathered such

83

a hefty, muscular, hairy son, such a horny son of the soil.... As for my daughter, she resembled her mother....

"*I found out later that my wife's father, who was forever in and out of the house, knew all that had been going on....*

"*Let me think now.... At the time I am about to speak of, Albert was twelve years old, and Lise eight....*

"*I was supposed to go to a concert at four o'clock with a friend who was the author of several books on the history of music.... But I found him ill in bed with bronchitis, so I returned home....*

"*Perhaps you are thinking of going to see the house? There's a small door cut into the big carriage gateway.... I had my key.... Instead of going through the hall, I went up the stairs on the right, which lead to the floor where the bedrooms are.... I intended to ask my wife to come with me...*"

Maigret jerked at the brass bellpull, and heard the clang of a heavy bell, as solemn as a convent bell. Footsteps. The footman, staring at him in astonishment.

"I should like to speak to the owners of this house, if you please."

"Which of the ladies do you want?"

"Whichever you like."

At this very moment, through a window on the ground floor, he caught sight of two women, both wearing garishly colored dressing gowns. One was smoking a cigarette in a long holder, the other a minute pipe. Maigret could not help smiling.

"What is it, Jean?"

A strong English accent. Both women were in their middle forties. The room, which must have been the main drawing room in the Forlacroixes' time, had been transformed into an artist's studio. Littered about were easels, extremely modernistic paintings, glasses and bottles, African and Chinese artifacts, in short, all the bric-à-brac of Montparnasse bohemianism.

Maigret proffered his card.

"Come in, Chief Superintendent. . . . We have not done anything amiss, I trust. . . . This is my friend, Mrs. Perkins. . . . I am Angelina Dodds. . . . Which of us do you want?"

She had great ease of manner, and a humorous twinkle in her eye.

"May I ask how long you have lived in this house?"

"Seven years . . . The previous owner was an elderly senator, who died. . . . Before him, we were told, the house used to belong to a judge."

What a pity the elderly senator had died. He, no doubt, had kept the house more or less as it had been in Forlacroix's time, since he had taken over the original furniture and some of the ornaments.

Now, a red-and-gold Chinese divan smothered in dragons clashed hideously with an exquisitely delicate Louis XVI pier glass.

Oh, well! A couple of English eccentrics, obviously, bitten with the painting bug, and dazzled by the glamour attached to Versailles.

"Do you employ a gardener?"

"Of course. Why do you ask?"

"I wonder if you would mind showing me the garden, or getting one of the servants to do so?"

Greatly intrigued, both of them went with him. It was a period garden, in keeping with the house, a replica, on a smaller scale, of the Trianon gardens.

"*I always looked after my rosebushes myself,*" the Judge had said. "*Which explains why I remembered the wells. . . .*"

There were three wells, and these were now pointed out to him. The one in the middle, which was filled in, was no doubt planted with geraniums or some other flowers in the summer.

"Would you mind very much if I had these wells dug up? It's bound to make a good deal of mess, and I haven't got the necessary authority to undertake the work without your consent."

"What are you looking for? Buried treasure?" exclaimed one of the Englishwomen, with a laugh. "Urbain! Come over here a minute, and bring a spade with you."

Far away in l'Aiguillon the Judge had spoken dispassionately, as though his story concerned someone other than himself.

"You know the term in flagrante delicto, *I daresay. . . . You must often have witnessed such scenes in hotel bedrooms and seedy lodgings. . . . There are cases. . . . What really got to me, I think, was that the man had such a coarse face, and that he looked at me with contempt. . . . And this in spite of his own appearance, clownish, loathsome, half naked, his hair all over the place, smudges of lipstick on his left cheek . . . I killed him. . . ."*

"Were you carrying a gun?"

"No, but I kept one in the chest of drawers in our bedroom. The drawer was within reach of my hand. . . . I did it in cold blood, I freely admit that. . . . I was more collected than I am now. . . . I thought of the children, who would soon be coming home from school. . . . I heard later that he was a café singer. . . . He wasn't at all handsome. . . . He had thick, greasy hair, all in a bunch at the back of his neck. . . ."

Maigret hastened up to the gardener.

"The topsoil goes down about ten inches, I suspect. Better get that out first. And underneath . . ."

"Stones and cement," declared Urbain.

"Well, whatever is there, it will have to be dug up."

The level voice had taken on a nightmare quality:

"I remembered the wells. . . . I carried the man and his clothes, and everything he had with him. . . . There wasn't much room in the well. I had to cram the body down into it, and even then I couldn't get it doubled up. . . . I covered it with big stones, and poured several sacks of cement over it. . . . But that isn't the real point. . . ."

It was at this juncture that the policeman's face had appeared, pressed against the window. The Judge, with a little shrug, had continued.

"From one minute to the next, my wife was transformed into a kind of Fury. In less than half an hour, Chief Superintendent, I heard from her own lips everything there was to know; the affairs she had had before our marriage, all her artful little tricks, her father's complicity. . . . Then followed a list of her many lovers, and details of her assignations with them. . . . She was unrecognizable. . . . She was literally foaming at the mouth. . . .

" 'And, as for this one, I loved him, do you hear me, I loved him!' she shrieked, with never a thought for the children, who had just come in, and might easily have heard.

"I should have sent for the police and told them the truth, shouldn't I? I would have been acquitted. But if I had, my children, and more especially my daughter, would have had to live out their lives knowing that their mother . . .

"Believe me, I thought it all out, although there was so little time. . . . It's amazing how clearly one sees things in moments of crisis. . . .

"I waited until nightfall. . . . It was the height of summer. . . . It didn't get dark until very late. . . . I'm tougher than I look. . . . And I seemed to find added strength that night. . . ."

•

87

Eleven o'clock. The ground, which had frozen during the night, was now moist and warm in the sunlight.

"Well?" asked Maigret.

"See for yourself."

The Chief Superintendent bent down. The digging had uncovered a whitish object. A skull.

"I do apologize, ladies, for all this mess. . . . But rest assured, I won't need to trouble you again. This has to do with a murder committed long ago. I will reimburse you for any expense incurred, pending your formal claim for compensation."

The Judge had not lied. He had killed a man. And for the best part of fifteen years, all knowledge of it had been kept from everyone except his wife, who now lived on the Riviera, in Nice, at the Villa des Roches-Grises with the Dutchman Horace Van Usschen, who had made his fortune in cocoa.

"Would you care for some whisky, Chief Superintendent?"

If there was one thing he couldn't abide, it was whisky. Still less could he endure the thought of discussing this case with anyone.

"I'll have to report this to the authorities. I'd like to get it over with before lunch."

"Will you be coming back?"

Assuredly not. This murder was no concern of his. What he was investigating was the death of a doctor named Janin in a house in l'Aiguillon.

Avenue de Paris sparkled in the all-pervasive sunlight, as if it had been sprinkled with gold dust. But time was pressing. He hailed a passing taxi.

"The Palais de Justice."

"It's no distance."

"What's that matter to you?"

He had himself announced, and was received with a mixture of skepticism and embarrassment.

He lunched alone, ordering himself a plate of *choucroute garnie* at the Brasserie Suisse. He read the newspaper without taking in a word.

"Waiter! Would you please put a call through for me to La Roche-sur-Yon forty-one. A priority call. Police business . . . Oh, and another to the prison . . ."

The beer was good, the *choucroute* tolerable, not bad at all, in fact. He ordered a couple more sausages. Not quite what the Sun King would have chosen perhaps, but who cared?

"Hello . . . Yes . . . She's settled in all right? . . . Splendid. What's that? . . . She's asking for a piano? . . . Hire one for her, then. . . . Yes, I do mean it. . . . I'll take the responsibility. . . . Her father will meet all expenses. . . . As for you, if you dare to leave your post, or if she manages to escape through the window . . ."

The prison authorities had nothing to report. At eleven that morning, Judge Forlacroix had been visited by his lawyer, who had spent half an hour in friendly conversation with his client.

7

Ask the Chief Superintendent

•

It was with real pleasure, at eight o'clock the next morning, that the Chief Superintendent went down the narrow little staircase, its varnished pine hardrail gleaming in the sunlight, to take his seat at his usual table in the deserted bar of the inn, and eat homemade sausage and freshly caught shrimp out of a thick pottery bowl.

"Thérèse!" he called out as he sat down. "My coffee . . ."

But it was the landlady who served him.

"Thérèse has gone to the butcher's."

"Tell me, madame, why is it that, although the tide is out, the harbor is deserted? Are the people around here afraid of the cold?"

"It's the neap tide," she replied.

"What does that mean?"

"The men don't go out to the mussel beds when the tides are slack."

"In other words, the mussel farmers have no work for half the year?"

"Not at all! Most of them own farmland, or market gardens or sheep and cattle."

Even Méjat, whom Maigret greeted warmly in spite of his

brilliantine, was wearing a scarf. It was green and much too bright, and made him look slightly ridiculous.

"Have a seat. . . . Have some breakfast. . . . And tell me what the poor old lady had to say."

He was referring to Marcel's mother. To tell the truth, Maigret was not sorry to have been able to unload that particular chore onto the Inspector.

"It's a typical, old-fashioned, local farmhouse, I suppose. Full of furniture, reminiscent of earlier times . . . And a grandfather clock with a sluggish brass pendulum winking in the firelight?"

"You've got it all wrong, Chief. The whole house gets a fresh coat of paint every year, and, in place of the old door, it has a new one, ornamented with fake wrought iron. The furniture comes from a department store on Boulevard Barbès."

"She began by offering you a drink, I suppose?"

"Yes."

"And you hadn't the heart to refuse."

Poor Méjat could not see that he had done anything wrong in accepting the proffered glass of aromatic, homemade plum brandy.

"There's no need to blush. . . . I wasn't getting at you."

Was he not, rather, thinking of himself, eating and drinking in the Judge's house?

"Some people are strong-minded enough to refuse, others are not. You went to see the old lady to pump her about her son, and you set the ball rolling by drinking her plum brandy. The Judge now, there's a man strong-minded enough to refuse, or so I believe. . . . To refuse anything . . . Even to himself . . . Don't look so puzzled. I'm just thinking aloud. Did she break down?"

"You've got to understand that she's almost as big and

beefy as her son. At first she tried to brazen it out, and then she changed her tack and became very highhanded. She said that if I went on badgering her, she would send for her lawyer. I asked her whether it was not true that her son had been absent from home for several days. That bothered her, I could see. After some hesitation, she said:

" 'I believe he's gone to Niort on business.'

" 'Niort? Are you sure of that? Did he spend the night there?'

" 'I don't know.'

" 'How can you say you don't know, with the two of you living alone under the same roof? Have I your permission to look around the house? I haven't got a warrant, but if you refuse . . .'

"We went upstairs. And there you really feel you are in an old house, with all that old-fashioned furniture, just as you described it, massive wardrobes and chests of drawers, and blown-up photographs on the walls.

" 'What does your son usually wear when he goes into town?'

"She took a blue serge suit from the wardrobe. I searched the pockets. I found this receipted bill from a hotel in Nantes. . . . Take a look at the date."

It was dated the fifth of January, a few days before Doctor Janin's arrival in l'Aiguillon.

"So you had no reason to regret that glass of plum brandy," remarked Maigret. He got up as he saw the telegraph boy arrive.

He resumed his seat with a handful of telegrams, and laid them on the table in front of him. As usual, he was in no hurry to open them.

"By the way, do you know why Didine and her husband, old Hulot, have such a grudge against the Judge? I had all sorts of fanciful notions about that, but it's quite simple really, like everything else in this village. The truth is as unadorned as that lighthouse out there, gleaming in the sun. Shortly after Hulot's retirement, the Judge came to live in l'Aiguillon. Didine went to see him and, reminding him that they had known one another as children, offered her services and those of her husband as cook and gardener respectively. Forlacroix, knowing the sort of woman she was, no doubt, refused. And that's all there is to it."

He opened one of the telegrams, read it, and handed it to Méjat.

NAVAL RATING MARCEL AIRAUD SERVED ABOARD MINE-SWEEPER VENGEUR.

"But seeing that the Judge has confessed . . ." protested Méjat.

"Oh, he's confessed, has he?"

"That's what it says in all the papers."

"And you, of course, believe everything you read in the papers!"

With exemplary patience, he whiled away the next ten hours, doing virtually nothing, roaming around among the beached fishing boats, while at the same time keeping an eye on the Judge's house. On two occasions, admittedly, he darted into the hotel for a quick nip, but only because it really was a very cold day.

He couldn't help smiling as he watched the two cars draw up one behind the other. Respect for the conventions was all very well, but this bordered on the ridiculous. The two men, who had set out from La Roche-sur-Yon at crack of dawn, were old friends. They had been on first-name terms since their school days. They would have much preferred to make the journey together in a single car. But, regrettably, one was the examining magistrate assigned to the l'Aiguillon murder investigation, and the other was the lawyer chosen by Judge Forlacroix to act for him. Having regard for the circumstances, they had endured hours of heart-searching the previous night. Should they or should they not?

Both men shook hands with Maigret. Maître Courtieux, a middle-aged man, was reputed to be the best lawyer in the locality.

"My client tells me that he entrusted all the keys of the house to you."

Maigret jingled them in his pocket, and the three men set off together for the house, where a policeman was still on guard outside. The Examining Magistrate remarked on this, not because he attached any particular importance to it, but because he wished it to be known that nothing escaped his notice.

"Strictly speaking, all the doors should have been sealed. . . . But seeing that Monsieur Forlacroix personally entrusted the keys to the Chief Superintendent, and that he has charge of them . . ."

It was really astonishing to observe the extent to which Maigret felt at home in that house. He made straight for the coat stand and, having hung up his coat, led the way to the library.

"As we shall be here some time, I propose to light the fire."

Maigret could not but feel moved at the sight of the two armchairs on either side of the fireplace, and the pipe ash and cigarette butts, which had not been cleared away.

"Do please make yourselves at home, gentlemen."

"My client's words to me," began the lawyer, sounding none too happy about it, "were, 'Ask the Chief Superintendent. He will tell you all you need to know.'

"So I am relying on you, Chief Superintendent, to tell us

94

just exactly what he did after having killed the man and walled him up, so to speak, in the well in his garden. . . ."

"You go first, Judge," murmured Maigret to the Examining Magistrate, as if this really were his home. "Mind you, I'm not expecting to make any sensational discoveries. I asked for a search warrant in the hope of being able to piece together an impression of Judge Forlacroix's life during the past few years.

"Note the refinement of taste with which every piece of furniture has been chosen, and the right place found for it, and, indeed, for every single ornament."

Forlacroix had not left Versailles immediately. Coldly and uncompromisingly, he had turned his wife out of the house, but not until he had written her a fairly substantial check.

Maigret could picture him very clearly, a small, emaciated figure, with his halo of unruly hair, neat, sensitive hands, and frigid manner. As the Chief Superintendent had previously remarked, he was not the man to be cajoled into compromise against his will. Didine had found this out, and, even after all these years, could not forget the cool indifference with which her proposition had been brushed aside, or, rather, not so much brushed aside as ignored.

"Did she not plead with you to allow her to remain with you and her children?" Maigret had asked, as they sat facing one another on either side of the hearth.

Of course! There had been more than one ugly scene. She had flung herself full-length on the floor. And for months afterward she had bombarded him with letters. She had begged. She had threatened.

"I never answered any of them. Then one day I learned that she had set up house on the Riviera with a Dutchman."

He had sold the house in Versailles. He had come to settle in l'Aiguillon. And then . . .

"Can't you feel the atmosphere in this house?" sighed Maigret. "It is redolent of comfort and the pleasures of easy living. And yet, for years on end, a man lived here tormented day after day by the thought that he was perhaps not the father of his own children. And the son, too, as he grew older, began to sense a mystery, and to ask questions about his mother and his birth."

He had just opened a door to a room filled with toys of every description, lying about as they had been left. In a corner stood a schoolboy's desk of unstained oak.

Next they came to Albert's former bedroom. There were still some of his old clothes hanging in the wardrobe. In another room they found a cupboard full of Lise Forlacroix's dolls.

"At the age of seventeen or eighteen," went on the Chief Superintendent, "Albert, for God knows what reason, conceived a violent dislike for his father. He couldn't understand why he kept his sister locked up. . . . This was just after Lise had had her first attack. . . .

"It was at about this time, also, that Albert came upon one of the letters written shortly after the breakup of the family. Hold on a minute . . . It must be in this desk. I have the key."

It seemed to him that he possessed not only the key to the Louis XIV writing desk, but also the key to all the characters whose interaction had caused so much damage over so many years. He puffed at his pipe as he led the Examining Magistrate and the lawyer from room to room. As he touched this or that object and broached this or that subject, he evinced a degree of delicacy unexpected in a man with such big hands and such a bulky frame.

"You can add it to the file," he said, without so much as glancing at it. "I know it by heart. She threatens her husband with prison. Albert demanded an explanation. Forlacroix refused to oblige. From then on they lived together like strangers. After his military service, Albert decided to make a life of his own, but something, unsatisfied curiosity perhaps, kept him in l'Aiguillon, and he set himself up as a mussel-gatherer. . . . You have seen him. . . . Despite his physique, he is restless and violent by temperament, a born rebel. As for the girl . . ."

There was a ring at the door. The Chief Superintendent went to open it. It was Méjat, delivering a telegram. Méjat was hoping to be invited in, but he was disappointed. Maigret returned upstairs and announced:

"I summoned her here by telegram. I have just had her reply. She is coming."

"Who?"

"Madame Forlacroix. She left Nice by car yesterday at noon."

Maigret's behavior was disturbing to watch. For something very strange indeed was happening. As he came and went in this house that was not his own, as he recalled events in the lives of people whose experiences he had not shared, he seemed no longer to be quite the same familiar Maigret, rough-hewn, bulky, and impassive, but unconsciously to have assumed some of the mannerisms and intonations of Judge Forlacroix. God knows, the two men could scarcely have been more dissimilar, and yet, at times, the resemblance was so striking that it made the Judge's lawyer feel uncomfortable.

"The first time I came to the house, Lise was in bed. . . . This bedside lamp here was switched on. . . . Forlacroix adored his daughter. . . . He adored her, and endured great anguish on her account, because, in spite of everything, he could never be sure . . . How could he even know for certain that she really was his child, and not that of some casual stranger, like the singer with the greasy hair?

"He loved her all the more because she was different from

97

other girls, because she needed him, and because she was impulsive and warm, like a kitten or a puppy.

"I fancy that, when she was not in the throes of an attack, she had all the spontaneous charm and grace of a six-year-old child.

"Her father consulted innumerable specialists. . . . I can tell you, gentlemen, that girls like Lise seldom live longer than sixteen or seventeen years. When they do, their condition deteriorates, the attacks recur more frequently, and they become sullen and withdrawn.

"Some of the village gossip can be taken with a pinch of salt, but it is nevertheless a fact that several men, two at least, took advantage of Lise before Marcel Airaud came on the scene. . . .

"And when he came into the picture . . ."

"One moment!" interposed the Examining Magistrate. "I have not yet had an opportunity of interrogating the accused. Does he claim to have been unaware of Marcel Airaud's nocturnal visits to his daughter?"

Maigret, who had been gazing out the window, continued to do so for a second or two, and then turned around.

"No."

An embarrassed silence.

"In other words, this man . . ." began the Magistrate.

The lawyer was beginning to wonder what on earth he could find to say in extenuation when pleading for this monster before the jurors of La Roche-sur-Yon.

"He knew what was going on," replied Maigret. "All the doctors were of the same opinion.

" 'Find her a husband! It's the only hope. . . .' "

"It's one thing to arrange a marriage for her, and another to tolerate the conduct of such a man as Airaud. . . ."

"Do you really imagine, Judge, that it's easy to find a

husband for a girl as severely handicapped as Lise? Forlacroix preferred to turn a blind eye. He resigned himself to the situation. After all, he must have realized that, in spite of that business with Thérèse, Airaud was a decent-enough boy. . . . I'll tell you more about that another time. . . . For the present, suffice it to say that Airaud also could not be sure that he was the father of his supposed child, although Thérèse has never ceased to nag him about it. Airaud was genuinely in love with Lise, so much so that he was ready to make her his wife in spite of everything. . . ."

Very deliberately, he tapped out the dottle of his pipe against his heel, and then said quietly:

"They were going to be married very shortly. . . ."

"What did you say?"

"I said that Marcel and Lise were due to be married in two months' time. If you knew Forlacroix better, you would understand. A man capable of resigning himself to the sort of life that he has led for many years past . . . He watched Marcel closely for a long time. . . . One day Airaud was going past the house when the front door opened. . . .

"Forlacroix, much to the alarm of the young man, appeared on the threshold. He murmured:

" 'I wonder if you could spare me a moment for a word in private?' "

Mechanically, Maigret set to work to wind one of the clocks, which had stopped.

"I know exactly how it must have happened, because I, too, have had the experience of chatting with him beside the fire. He would have been very matter-of-fact about it. Very deliberately, he poured the drinks, port served in his best glasses. . . . He said . . . He said everything that needed to be said. He told the whole truth about Lise.

"Airaud, very much shaken, did not know what to say. . . .

He asked for a few days to think it over.... His answer would have been 'Yes,' of that there is no doubt. I daresay you have experience of men like him, Judge, whose physical strength is equaled by their simplicity of mind? One often sees such men at country markets.... You know how they conduct their business.

"I'm telling you as a fact that Airaud decided to consult the former ship's surgeon who had served with him aboard the *Vengeur,* with whom he had perhaps struck up a friendship.... He set out for Nantes...."

The sound of a car horn. A series of prolonged blasts, out of the blue. Through the window could be seen a luxurious car, driven by a uniformed chauffeur, who got out and went to open the passenger door.

Maigret and his companions were in Lise's sitting room, where the piano was kept. All three stood watching at the window.

"Horace Van Usschen!" announced Maigret, pointing to an old man, who was the first to get out. He moved stiffly, like an automaton, as if his joints needed greasing.

A little crowd of spectators had gathered at the corner of the street. Van Usschen was certainly a quaint-enough spectacle, in his light flannel suit, white shoes, voluminous checked overcoat, and white cloth cap. His appearance would undoubtedly have caused no stir on the Riviera, but it created a sensation in l'Aiguillon, where even the summer visitors were quite humble people.

He had a look of old John D. Rockefeller about him, and he was certainly no less wrinkled and emaciated. He leaned into the car and stretched out his hand. And it was then that an enormous woman came into view. She was swathed in furs, and she subjected the house to a very searching look. Then she spoke to the chauffeur, and he went up to the door and rang the bell.

"With your permission, gentlemen, I think we'll leave the Dutchman out of it. For the time being, at least . . ."

He went to open the door, and saw at a glance that the Judge had not exaggerated. Valentine Forlacroix, née Constantinesco, had been a beautiful woman. Even now she had fine eyes, and, in spite of some drooping at the corners, a full, sensual mouth, very like Lise's.

"Well, here I am!" she announced. "Come along, Horace."

"Pardon me, madame, but for the time being I would prefer to see you alone. . . . Indeed, it might be to your advantage as well, don't you think?"

Horace, looking somewhat put out, returned to the car, wrapped himself in a rug, and sat motionless, seemingly oblivious of the children who peered in at him through the windows.

"You know your way about the house. . . . With your permission, I suggest we make ourselves comfortable in the library, where there is a fire."

Following him into the room, she protested:

"I can't see what all this can possibly have to do with me! Admittedly the man is my husband, but it's no concern of mine what crimes he may have committed. Considering how long we have lived apart, you can't expect me to take any interest in his recent activities."

The Examining Magistrate and the lawyer had, meanwhile, joined them downstairs.

"His Honor the Examining Magistrate will tell you that we are not concerned with his recent activities, but with events that involved both of you, when you were still living together."

A pungent scent was gradually seeping into every corner of the room. Valentine Forlacroix stretched out a hand loaded with rings and tipped with blood-red nails, and took a cigarette from the box on the table. She looked about her for matches.

Maigret lit one and held it out to her.

The Examining Magistrate felt that the time had come for him to have his say.

"As you are no doubt aware, madame, a legal obligation rests upon anyone witnessing the commission of a crime, even if that person is in no way involved, to inform the authorities, on pain of prosecution."

She was a cool customer all right! Forlacroix had told no lie. Puffing steadily at her cigarette, she took her time. Her mink coat had fallen open, to reveal a black silk dress adorned with a diamond clip. She paced up and down the long room, stopped in front of the fire, picked up the tongs and returned a fallen log to its place.

Then she turned to face them, as if realizing that the time for playacting was past. She was braced for a fight. Her eyes had lost some of their sparkle, but none of their sharpness. Her lips were compressed.

"Very well!" she said, sitting down and leaning her elbow on the table. "I'm ready to listen to what you have to say. As for you, Chief Superintendent, you can hardly expect me to thank you for having caught me in your trap."

"What's she talking about?" asked the Examining Magistrate, turning to Maigret with a puzzled frown.

"I'd hardly call it a trap," growled Maigret, extinguishing his pipe with his thumb. "I telegraphed to madame asking her to come here and tell us why she had visited her husband a month or so ago. . . . And indeed, Your Honor, that is precisely the question that I should be obliged if you would put to her in the first place."

"You heard that, madame? I must warn you that, in the absence of my clerk, this interview is off the record, and that Maître Courtieux here is your husband's legal representative."

With a look of contempt she blew out a cloud of smoke and shrugged.

"I wanted to discuss divorce," she said.

"Why now rather than years ago?"

The transformation described by Forlacroix occurred before their very eyes. From one second to the next, this diamond-studded woman coarsened perceptibly. It was embarrassing to watch.

"Because Van Usschen is sixty-eight years old, don't you see?" she admitted brazenly.

"And you wanted him to marry you?"

"He decided on it six months ago, when his nephew begged him to bail him out, after having lost some hundreds of thousands of francs at roulette."

"So you decided to come here. Was your husband prepared to receive you?"

"He wouldn't let me past the entrance hall."

"What did he say?"

"That he didn't recognize my existence, and therefore could see no point in divorcing me."

This response, so typical of Forlacroix, delighted Maigret. Hitherto, he had left the floor to the Examining Magistrate, but he now scribbled a note in pencil on a scrap of paper, and passed it to him.

"What did you do next?"

"I went back to Nice."

"Just a minute! Didn't you call on someone else in l'Aiguillon?"

"What do you mean?"

"Your son, for instance."

She glowered at the Chief Superintendent.

"Talk about a snoop! Yes, as a matter of fact I did, as it happened, meet my son."

"As it happened?"

"I went to see him."

"Did he recognize you, after all those years?"

She shrugged.

"What does it matter? I told him that Forlacroix was not his father."

"Are you sure of that?"

"How can one ever be sure? . . . I told him that I wanted a divorce, and that my husband wouldn't hear of it. I told him he was a cruel man with a heavy load on his conscience, and that if he, Albert, could persuade him to change his mind about the divorce . . ."

"In other words, you wanted to get your son on your side. Did you offer him money?"

"He wouldn't take it."

"Did he promise to help you?"

She nodded.

"Did you tell him about that other murder?"

"No . . . All I said was that, if I chose, I could get Forlacroix put away for a very long time."

"Did you write to him subsequently?"

"Yes. To ask whether he'd made any progress."

"Have you ever heard the name Doctor Janin?"

"Never!"

The Examining Magistrate looked inquiringly at Maigret, who murmured:

"If madame is tired, we might perhaps adjourn for lunch? I fancy Monsieur Van Usschen will be getting impatient, out there in the car."

"Am I under arrest?"

"Not yet," declared the Magistrate. "For the present, I will only ask you to keep yourself available in case you are needed. I should be grateful, for instance, if you could let me have your address in La Roche-sur-Yon."

"Very well. The Hôtel des Deux Cerfs . . . I believe it's the best."

They all stood up. In parting, she smiled at the Examining Magistrate and the lawyer, but could scarcely restrain herself from making a face at Maigret, or putting out her tongue at him. Maigret, looking very pleased with himself, relit his pipe.

8

A Meal of Baked Potatoes

"Ace, king, queen of trumps."

"That won't help you. I have a pair and a ten. That makes fifty."

"We'll see about that! Your fifty may still be beaten."

What time was it? The advertising clock on the wall had stopped. The lights had been switched on for some time. The room was hot. The little glasses had already been refilled three or four times, and the smell of marc was mingled with the fumes of pipe smoke.

"No matter! I'll lead my trump," declared Maigret, putting down a card.

"It's the best thing you can do, Chief Superintendent. . . . Even if it's backed up by the nine. . . ."

They were playing for a thousand points for the fourth or fifth time. Maigret was smoking, leaning back a little in his chair. His partner was the landlord, and the other pair were fishermen, one of them the old eel catcher Bariteau.

Méjat, sitting astride his chair, was watching the play.

"There! I knew you had the nine. . . ."

"Hey, Méjat, do you happen to remember the name of the police surgeon?"

"I made a note of it in my book."

"Be a good fellow, then, and give him a call. Ask him if he can let me know approximately how long before he died the man had his last meal, and whether it was a full meal or a snack. . . . Do you understand?"

"Who was it who had fifty points? And thirty-six . . ."

The innkeeper was adding up the score. Maigret, to all appearances, was wallowing in the warmth of the cozy fire, and if anyone had suddenly asked him what he was thinking, he himself would have been surprised at his own thoughts.

He was far away from the present, back in the days of the Bonnot case, when he had been thin and had sported a waxed mustache and a little pointed beard, and worn four-inch-high starched collars and a top hat.

"You can take it from me, young fellow," his boss, Chief Superintendent Xavier Guichard, later to become chief commissioner of the Police Judiciaire, had said to him. "All this talk of flair"—the newspapers at that time were full of stories of his remarkable flair—"is just a publicity stunt."

"In any criminal investigation, what really matters is evidence, the collection of well-substantiated facts on which a case can be built, and which will stand up, come what may.

"From then on, it's simply a matter of plodding on, slowly but surely, like a man with a wheelbarrow. It's a question of professional competence, and when people talk of flair, all they really mean is luck. . . ."

Strange as it might seem, it was the recollection of this conversation that had prompted him to make a fourth at cards, much to the amazement of Méjat.

First, Valentine Forlacroix and the Dutchman had driven off in their car, soon to be followed by the Examining Magistrate and the lawyer in theirs. Maigret, left alone, had stood in the middle of the road for a minute or two, seemingly at a loss. Forlacroix was in prison. His daughter, Lise, was in a nursing home. Before leaving, the Examining Magistrate had officially sealed up the house. He had left feeling pleased with himself, as if he had captured a great prize. Everything was now in his hands, and his alone. It was he who, in his chambers in the Palais de Justice at La Roche-sur-Yon, would conduct the interrogations and arrange the confrontations.

"So that's it!" Maigret had mumbled to himself, as he returned to the hotel.

Why should he be feeling so disgruntled? Matters were merely taking their normal course. This feeling, almost of envy, was really too absurd.

"What do we do now, Chief?"

Didine and her husband . . . Marcel Airaud . . . Thérèse . . . Albert Forlacroix . . .

"Whom do we tackle first?"

Maigret had started by taking a hand at cards.

"I lead with trumps."

"Then I'll play my eight."

At one point, while his partner was adding up the score, he had taken a pencil and notebook from his pocket and, though he hardly ever made a note, he wrote, pressing so hard that he snapped the lead:

"*Doctor Janin arrived in l'Aiguillon on Tuesday, on the four-thirty bus.*"

This was the first established fact, as Xavier Guichard would have said. And then? The next fact was that the same Janin had been killed that night in the Judge's house. But on this point, there was less certainty. Three days having elapsed before the autopsy, the police surgeon had been unable to establish the time of death to within less than a few hours. And there was no proof that . . .

On Wednesday morning, Janin's body was seen lying on the floor of the fruit loft in the Judge's house.

"Hearts are trumps. . . . Agreed?" his partner asked, puzzled by his absent-minded stare.

"Hearts it is! Whose turn to play?"

Out of respect for him, the landlord forbore to make the customary retort:

"The idiot who's asking."

From then on, Maigret's eyes kept wandering to the two scribbled sentences that represented the only incontrovertible facts in the case.

Méjat could be heard speaking on the telephone, for which purpose he assumed a quite hideous falsetto.

"Well?"

"The doctor had to reread his report. . . . According to the contents of the stomach, the dead man had eaten a full meal. . . . There were substantial amounts of alcohol."

Though Méjat could not think why, this information appeared to cause Maigret great satisfaction. He tilted his chair farther back, so that he had to clutch at the table to prevent himself from falling over.

"Well, well!" he exclaimed, after having studied his cards. "So the fellow ate a hearty meal, did he?"

Maybe it was nothing to write home about. And yet . . . Janin had not dined at the Hôtel du Port or at the little inn across the road, and they were the only two restaurants in l'Aiguillon.

"I have a run of three."

"What's your highest card?"

"The king . . . By the way, am I right in thinking that young Forlacroix owns a truck?"

"He does, but it's been out of action for the last fortnight."

There was no evidence to show that Janin had been driven anywhere by anyone. So, if he had had a meal . . .

"Méjat, I want you to go to the butcher's. . . . I say, landlord, am I right in thinking that there's only one butcher in this village?"

"Yes, and he only slaughters once a week."

"Ask him if anyone came into his shop on that Tuesday, between four and seven, to buy something a bit special."

"Who?"

"Anyone at all."

Méjat got into his overcoat and, with a sigh, set off. The opening and shutting of the door let in a stream of cold air that nipped at their legs. Thérèse sat beside the stove, knitting. No sooner was the door shut than it was opened again. Méjat stood in the doorway, making signs to the Chief Superintendent.

"What do you want?"

"Could I have a word with you, Chief?"

"One moment . . . Trumps! . . . Clubs take all. . . . And you can't beat my ace of diamonds. . . . I have all the tricks, gentlemen!"

Then, to Méjat:

"What is it?"

"It's Didine. . . . She's outside, wanting to speak to you. . . . She says it's very urgent."

"Thérèse, get me my hat and coat. . . . And you stand in for me for a few minutes, Méjat, will you?"

Before going out, he lit his pipe. It was a dark night, and there was a hard frost. Few lights were showing, apart from that in the window of the grocer's shop, which was dimmed by the semiopaque advertising stickers plastered all over it. The shadowy little figure of Didine seemed to merge with that of the Chief Superintendent.

"Come with me. . . . Don't walk beside me. . . . If you keep a few paces behind me, no one will know that we're together."

She was carrying a half-empty bag, and, in her other hand, a small sickle, such as old countrywomen use to cut grass for their rabbits. Presently, they came to Albert Forlacroix's house. A shadowy figure moved in the darkness. It was the

110

policeman on guard, greeting Maigret with a smart, military salute.

Every now and then Didine turned around to make sure the Chief Superintendent was following, then, suddenly, she disappeared into a black gap between two houses, as if the walls had closed on her like a pair of jaws. He followed her into this gap. An icy hand touched his.

"Watch out for barbed wire!"

By daylight, no doubt, the place was ordinary enough, but in the dark, led by that strange little witchlike creature with her bag and her sickle, Maigret felt disoriented. He stumbled on a pile of oyster shells, then his nostrils were assailed by a powerful smell of garbage cans.

"There's a wire fence here. . . . You'll have to climb over."

The crunch of frozen cabbages. He was in a kitchen garden at the back of the houses. It was one of several, separated by rusting strands of wire. Something moved, something alive: rabbits in a hutch.

"I come here to cut grass for my rabbits," she said, still leading the way.

The village consisted, in fact, of no more than a single, continuous row of houses, with vegetable gardens at the back. Beyond them was a ditch, into which the sea water flowed at high tide, and then marshland as far as the eye could see.

"Don't make a sound. . . . Don't talk. . . . Watch where you put your feet. . . ."

She was leading him by the hand, and presently they were creeping along beside a whitewashed wall. A shadowy figure was just discernible close to a faintly lighted window. As they drew nearer, he recognized Didine's customs officer, with his finger to his lips.

He would have been hard put to it to say what he had been expecting, but, whatever it was, it was certainly not the scene that now confronted him: a peaceful rural interior, as in an old farmhouse print left hanging over the fireplace from generation to generation.

Justin Hulot had stepped aside to make way for him at the window, which was so low that he had to stoop a little to see into the room. Through the glass, he could see a lighted stable lantern, standing on a barrel, which cast a yellowish glow.

Maigret had already realized that they must be just behind Albert Forlacroix's house. What he was seeing was the interior of a shed of sorts, located at the back of the yard, such as is commonly found in rural areas, and is normally used for storing empty barrels, cooking pots, rusty old tools, sacks, crates, and bottles.

In the fireplace, used no doubt to boil the feed for the livestock and, at Christmastime, to roast the pig, a few logs were burning.

There were two men in front of the fire, one sitting on a crate, the other on an upturned basket. Both were wearing those thigh-length rubber boots, turned down to the knee, which always, for Maigret, evoked a mental picture of the Three Musketeers.

Both were tall and heavily built, and both young. Two giants in fancy dress. Actually, they were wearing the traditional garments of the mussel-gatherer, but in that light they looked more like figures in a Rembrandt painting.

One of the men took a cigarette from his pocket and handed it to the other, who lit it from a piece of smoldering wood from the fire.

They were talking. Their lips could be seen moving, but, unfortunately, not a sound could be heard.

One of the two men, the one who had produced the cigarette, and who was now lighting one for himself, was Albert Forlacroix. The other, huddled very close to the fire, was Marcel Airaud, though he was scarcely recognizable with a golden beard of several days' growth.

Didine's skinny body brushed against Maigret as she whispered:

"They were already there an hour ago, when I first looked. It was not quite dark then. Young Forlacroix slipped out for a moment to fetch some potatoes."

He could make nothing of this reference to potatoes, which seemed to him preposterous at such a time.

"I didn't like to come into the bar. I did tap on the window several times, but you were so absorbed in your game of cards that you didn't notice."

What did she expect, scratching away like a mouse? Then, having failed to attract his attention, she had scampered off home, and sent her husband to mount guard.

Had she first chanced to look in through the window while cutting grass for her rabbits in Albert Forlacroix's back garden? If not, what could possibly have brought her there? He was puzzled and a little uneasy. Her husband had stepped back a few paces, and was waiting in the shadows.

"I felt sure he'd come back," she added.

"And that he would make straight for Albert Forlacroix?"

"Shhh!"

Maigret never could manage to keep his voice down, so he judged it wiser to remain silent.

"Are you going to arrest them both?" she whispered.

He did not reply. He did not move. Behind them, the beam of the Baleines lighthouse swept the sky, around and around endlessly, and now and then a cow mooed in the marshes. Presumably they were still playing cards at the Hôtel du Port, and Thérèse, no doubt, was beginning to feel uneasy at Maigret's continued absence.

As to the two men ... The Chief Superintendent had not

noticed until now how much alike they were in appearance.

They both followed the same calling, exposed to salt water, spray, and sea air, and this showed in the healthy pink glow of their skin, and their bleached hair.

Both were heavily built and lumbering, as men are whose lives are a ceaseless struggle against the tireless forces of nature.

They smoked. They talked peaceably. They gazed into the fire. Presently Marcel, an expression of artless enjoyment on his face, poked about among the embers with an iron rod.

He said something to his friend, who got up, went across to the low door, and had to duck to go through it. He returned a few minutes later with a couple of thick glasses, which he proceeded to fill straight out of a barrel standing in a corner of the room.

White wine! Never in his life had Maigret so longed for a glass of white wine. It looked so delicious. As for the potatoes . . . For potatoes there were, just as the old woman had said . . .

They brought back so many childhood memories, recalling illustrations in the books of James Fenimore Cooper and Jules Verne. Here they were in France, in the very heart of a French village, and yet they could be thousands of miles away. The two men could just as easily have been Canadian trappers, or castaways on a desert island. Their working clothes were timeless. Marcel's stiff, bushy beard lent color to the illusion.

For what he was raking out of the embers with his iron rod was a scattering of big potatoes, blackened and piping hot, and the charred skin crumbled between his thick fingers, to reveal the smoking yellow flesh beneath. He bit into one.

Once again, his companion rose to his feet. His head almost touched the ceiling. A string of sausages hung from a nail above the hearth. He took a knife from his pocket, and cut two from the string.

"What are they doing?" whispered Didine.

He did not answer. He would have given much to have been able to share that makeshift meal of potatoes baked in the embers of the fire, sausages browned from long hanging in the smoke, and cool wine from the wood.

The most disturbing aspect of the scene was the relaxed and easy manner of the two young fellows, who were far from imagining that their every action was being spied upon, even down to the smallest movement of their lips.

What could they be saying to one another? There they were, utterly self-reliant, each confident that the other could be trusted. Crouching over the fire, they ate with their clasp knives, as countryfolk and sailors do everywhere. There was nothing fevered in their interchanges. One or the other occasionally dropped a word or two, and then fell silent.

"Aren't you going to arrest them?"

Maigret gave a start, feeling something brush against his leg. But it was only a dog, a small terrier of some sort, little more than a puppy, belonging to one of the neighbors, probably. It nuzzled against him, not making a sound.

"Justin!" hissed Didine.

She pointed to the dog, which might start yapping at any moment. The customs officer seized it by the scruff of the neck and removed it.

Yet the two men could not be said to be in high spirits. They were not uneasy, but neither were they particularly cheerful. There was an air of oppressive tranquillity about the scene. Albert got up and cut down some more sausages. Then he turned toward the window and, for a second or two, Maigret thought that he had caught sight of him. But he had seen nothing.

Presently, they wiped their mouths and lit fresh cigarettes. Airaud yawned. Since he knew that the police were hot on his heels, how long was it since he had last had any sleep? He picked his teeth with the point of his knife, and rested his head against the wall.

Once again, young Forlacroix left the room. This time he was away much longer, and Maigret was just beginning to grow anxious when he reappeared, kicking the door open with his foot. He was heavily laden. On his head, he carried a mattress folded in half and a pile of bed linen, and, under his arm, a pillow. Marcel went across to assist. They showed themselves to be surprisingly concerned with cleanliness. Airaud fetched an old stable broom which was propped in a corner, and swept the beaten earth floor before the mattress was laid on it.

The customs officer, having got rid of the dog, had returned to his post, and was waiting without any visible sign of impatience.

"Aren't you going to arrest them?" hissed Didine once more. She was by now shivering with cold.

Airaud divested himself of his oilskin jacket, and sat down on the floor to take off his boots. They watched him as he removed his socks and, with surprising care and deliberation, rubbed his swollen feet. His companion said something to him. Was he offering to bring hot water to bathe his feet? Maigret felt sure he was. Marcel stood up again and stretched, before lying down full length on the mattress with a sigh so deep that it could almost be heard from outside.

Albert Forlacroix picked up the stable lantern and glanced around the room. He frowned as he caught sight of the window. Had he forgotten about it? Of course not! Reassuringly, he reminded himself that there was nothing but marshland beyond.

Now there was an odd thing! He slapped his guest hard on the top of his tousled head. Then, slinging the lantern from his wrist, he stirred his tall, bulky frame and went out, closing the door behind him.

Maigret beckoned Didine aside.

"Is there a back way out of the house?" he asked.

She pointed to the low wall surrounding Forlacroix's back yard.

He decided that he could safely leave the customs officer to keep guard. He picked his way back among the oyster shells, the garbage cans and broken bottles, parted from Didine in the street, and went into the police station.

He returned with a policeman, and instructed him to relieve Hulot. Didine was still out there in the street, with her sickle and her bag half full of grass. She was looking at him with a decidedly quizzical expression, or so it seemed to him.

"Well, what have you to say? If you ask me, if it wasn't for old Didine . . . How many of your policemen have you had running around in circles looking for him? Policemen!"

She laughed contemptuously.

"But nobody bothers to come and see me, and yet I could . . ."

"Go on home," he urged. "I'll come and see you, tonight . . . or tomorrow."

"Or when the moon is blue!" she retorted cynically. "Come along, Justin. You'll see! Even now, I bet they find some way of keeping them out of prison."

The policeman on duty outside Albert Forlacroix's house was no longer lurking in the shadows, but was standing in the middle of the road.

"Has he gone out?" asked Maigret.

"Look over there. You see that dark shape just beyond the

117

third gas lamp? That's him. . . . He's going into the hotel bar."

A few minutes later, Maigret followed him there. The card game was still in progress. Méjat, as might have been expected, was disputing every point.

"I tell you, gentlemen, that since it was my call . . . I appeal to you, Chief. . . . If I play hearts when . . ."

Albert Forlacroix was sitting all alone at a long table which could comfortably have accommodated ten. He was following the game from a distance. Thérèse had brought him a mug of white wine, but he seemed in no hurry to drink it.

"Well, I'll be damned!" grunted Maigret, recalling the wine drawn from the wood, and the potatoes and sausages.

"Will you take over, Chief?"

"Not just now. You carry on."

He did not take off his coat. He was feeling his way, and keeping a wary eye on the young man, who was sitting there with his long legs stretched out in front of him.

Was he really feeling up to it? Could he muster the necessary determination? Once he had set things in motion, he would have to go on to the end, whatever the cost. The advertising clock was still out of order. He looked at his watch. It was seven o'clock. Thérèse was laying the tables.

Should he have his dinner first? Or would it be better . . . ?

"Bring me a half-bottle of white wine, Thérèse," he called out.

But it would be a poor substitute for the white wine that those two had been drinking.

Albert Forlacroix gazed pensively at him.

"I say, Méjat . . ."

"Yes, Chief? Sorry . . . I forgot to declare my run of three."

"It's a winner!"

"What about the butcher?"

"I've just seen him. . . . I put the question to him, but he

118

can't remember. He claims that if anyone had been in at that time of day, asking for something especially choice, he would have remembered."

He was going around in circles. He was still feeling his way. He went down the two steps leading to the kitchen, and lifted the lids of the saucepans.

"What are you giving us for dinner, madame?"

"Calves' liver *à la bourgeoise* . . . I hope you like it? I didn't think to ask you."

That settled it. He could not abide liver in any form.

"See here, Méjat, when you've finished your game, I want you to come with me to the town hall. Is the stove still going?"

"It was, earlier."

The time had come at last. He went up to Albert Forlacroix.

"Would you mind if we had a little chat? Not here. In my office. You've had your dinner, I take it?"

The young man stood up without a word.

"All right, let's go."

And the two of them went out together into the night.

9

The Interrogation

•

Any one of his staff at the Quai des Orfèvres, Lucas or Janvier, for instance, would have recognized the signs at a glance. Even his back was eloquent. Was that a hump between those hunched shoulders? At any rate, if that back had been seen in the long corridors of Police Headquarters, Maigret's inspectors would have exchanged glances. And if, later, Maigret, without offering any explanation, had summoned a man to his office, they would have murmured:

"Hm. He's in for it!"

And it would have been no surprise to them, two or three hours later, to see the waiter from the Brasserie Dauphine arriving with a tray of sandwiches and beer.

But here, there was no one to see Maigret and his companion walking along the dark street.

"Hold on a second, will you?"

The Chief Superintendent went into the little general store, which was full of strange smells, and bought some coarse tobacco and a box of matches.

"And I'll have a pack of strong cigarettes as well. . . . No, on second thought, you'd better make it two packs."

In a jar, all stuck together, were the kind of candies that

120

had been his childhood favorites, but he hadn't the nerve to buy some for himself. As they walked along, Albert Forlacroix was silent, visibly making an effort to appear unconcerned.

The wrought-iron gate, the forecourt of the town hall, and, as he opened his office door, a welcoming gust of warm air from the stove, which glowed red in the dark.

"Come in, Forlacroix. . . . Make yourself at home."

Maigret switched on the lights, took off his coat and hat, and refilled the stove. Then he began pacing up and down the room, and, as he did so, a faint flicker of anxiety crossed his face from time to time. He paced back and forth, his glance resting on this object or that; he moved things about, smoked, and grumbled, and generally behaved as if he were waiting for something which eluded him.

And that something was inspiration, though he preferred to call it a sense of well-being.

"Take a seat. . . . You may smoke if you wish."

He noted that Forlacroix followed the rural custom of keeping an open pack of cigarettes in his jacket pocket and pulling out a single cigarette whenever he wanted one. He did so now, and Maigret lit a match for him. Then, just as he, too, was about to sit down, his glance rested on the window, and he went over to it, intending to close the shutters. He could not get the window to open, however, so he had to content himself with pulling down the dusty blind.

"Well, here we are," he said, with a sigh of satisfaction, and sat down. "Now, what have you got to tell me, Forlacroix?"

The "grilling," as they would say at the Quai des Orfèvres, was about to begin. Albert did not trust the Chief Superintendent an inch. Leaning well back in his chair to allow more room for his long legs, he looked searchingly at Maigret, making no attempt to conceal his resentment.

121

"Was it you who sent for my mother?" he asked, after a brief silence.

So he must have seen her, either as she was getting out of the car or as she was leaving the house. He must, therefore, also have seen the Dutchman, Horace Van Usschen.

"Your mother's testimony was indispensable," replied Maigret. "At present, she is staying in La Roche-sur-Yon, where she will no doubt remain for several days. You may, perhaps, wish to go and see her?"

And, looking searchingly at the young man, he thought:

You, my boy, are as irrationally devoted to your mother as you are bitterly hostile to your father, or, rather, to the man who passes for your father.

Then suddenly, without preamble:

"Am I right in thinking that when you last saw your mother, she confirmed that Forlacroix was not your father?"

"I knew that already," growled Albert, staring down at his boots.

"And for a very long time, if I'm not mistaken . . . Let's see now . . . how old would you have been when you first found out? It must have been very distressing for you."

"Quite the reverse!"

"So you hated Judge Forlacroix even before that?"

"I certainly didn't like him."

He was a cautious fellow. He was weighing his words with characteristic peasant wariness and, whatever his feelings might be, he was careful not to get carried away, perhaps because he knew the ferocity of his own temper.

"How old were you when . . . ?"

"About sixteen. I was at school in Lucon. I was kept at home for several days. . . . My father—Forlacroix, I mean— had sent for a well-known medical specialist from Paris. I thought, at first, he'd come to see my sister, but, in fact, it was for both of us. . . ."

122

"Was your sister . . . odd . . . even then?"

"She wasn't quite like other girls."

"And you?"

Albert started violently, then, looking Maigret straight in the eye, said:

"No one has ever accused me of abnormality. I did extremely well at school. The doctor examined me for hours on end. He took swabs, and samples of blood and urine. The Judge was there in the room with us. He seemed anxious and overwrought. He kept asking incomprehensible questions, mainly on the subject of blood groups, group A, group B. . . . He waited impatiently for several days for the results of the tests, and when, at last, a letter arrived from a pathologist in Paris, he subjected me to an icy stare, and gave a frigid little smile, as if he felt he had at last been relieved of a heavy burden. . . ."

Albert spoke slowly, weighing his words.

"I questioned some of the older boys at school. I learned that a child's blood group is always the same as that of a parent, and that, in some countries, blood tests are admitted as evidence in paternity suits. . . . Well, my blood group turned out to be different from that of the Judge."

He said this almost gloatingly.

"I toyed with the idea of running away, but I had no money. . . . I would have liked to have gone to my mother, but I had no idea where to find her, and the Judge always shut up like a clam whenever I mentioned her name. I served my time in the army. . . . And when I was released, I decided to come back here, and make a living in the same way as most other people hereabouts. . . ."

"You realized, I suppose, that you were best suited by temperament to a life of hard physical labor? But, tell me, what made you decide to settle in the same village as the Judge?"

123

"On account of my sister . . . I rented a house, and started working in the mussel beds. I went to see the Judge, and demanded that he should hand over my sister to me."

"And he refused, of course!"

"Why do you say 'of course'?"

Once again, he was looking sullen and resentful.

"Because it's plain to me that the Judge worships his daughter."

"Or hates her," muttered Albert between his teeth.

"Do you really believe that?"

"At any rate, he hated me."

He stood up abruptly.

"What has all this got to do with your inquiries? It's just a trick to make me talk, isn't it?"

He fumbled in his pocket for a cigarette, but found he had none left. Maigret held out one of the packs he had bought for just such a contingency.

"Sit down, Forlacroix."

"Is it true that the Judge has confessed?"

"Confessed to what?"

"You know very well what I mean."

"He has confessed to a murder committed long ago. Years ago, in Versailles, he caught your mother in bed with a man. He killed that man. . . ."

"Oh!"

"Tell me, Forlacroix . . ."

A long silence, during which Maigret stared broodingly at him.

"Is Marcel Airaud a friend of yours?"

Another long silence. As was his wont, the Mayor had provided a couple of bottles of wine. Maigret leaned across the table, and poured himself a glass.

"What's that got to do with you?"

124

"Nothing . . . Not much, at any rate . . . But you are roughly the same age. And he, like you, is a mussel-gatherer. . . . You must have seen a good deal of him, at work, at the local dances and what not. . . . I'm referring to the days before he began visiting your sister at night."

"We used to be friends, yes."

"You live alone, don't you? It seems very strange to me that a young man of your age should have such a taste for solitude. Your house is big enough."

"I have a woman in every day to do the cleaning."

"I know. And what about your meals? You don't mean to tell me that you do your own cooking."

Albert Forlacroix, glowering, wondered what on earth the Chief Superintendent was getting at.

"Sometimes I do. I'm not fussy. A slice of ham, a couple of eggs . . . a few oysters for starters . . . Occasionally I have a meal at the Hôtel du Port."

"It seems odd."

"What does?"

"Nothing . . . You. In effect, you live in l'Aiguillon just as if you were miles away from civilization. Have you never considered getting married?"

"No."

"What about your friend Airaud?"

"He's not my friend."

"True, he is *no longer* your friend. In short, you and he quarreled when rumors began flying about that he was in the habit of spending the night with your sister. Am I right?"

By now, Forlacroix's uneasiness was beginning to show in his face. At the beginning, although he had been on his guard, he had not attached any great importance to Maigret's questions. But now, suddenly, he felt as if he were becoming entangled in a web of fine threads.

What had the Chief Superintendent in mind? Maigret poured him a drink, and pushed the pack of cigarettes toward him.

"Have a drink. Have a cigarette. Make yourself comfortable. . . . We have a great deal to discuss."

Albert's response to this could be read in his face as plainly as if he had spoken:

I won't say another word! I refuse to answer any more questions!

Maigret got up and began wandering around the room again. He stood for some time contemplating the bust of the Republic.

"Are you hungry?"

"No!"

"Perhaps you have already had dinner? I must confess *I'm* ravenous. I wish I'd thought of bringing along a few baked potatoes. . . ."

That's right! That's right! Shake in your shoes, boy. Still, you're a cool customer; everyone knows that.

"Fine, upstanding fellows that you are, you and Airaud, I suppose, are looked upon as a pair of cockerels in the hen roost. . . . All the girls are after you, I don't doubt. . . ."

"I'm not interested in girls."

"But Airaud is. . . . He's even fathered a child on one of them. You must have been furious when you found out he was your sister's lover. I'm surprised there wasn't more of an explosion. . . ."

"We did come to blows."

"More than once, I'll bet . . . Because it didn't stop. . . . That puzzles me. . . . I hardly know him. . . . You know much more about him than I do. . . . Has it ever occurred to you that Marcel might be genuinely in love with your sister?"

"I haven't the slightest idea of that."

"So, at any rate, some people are saying. The story is that he intended to marry her, and that the Judge had given his consent. In that event, I presume, you would have buried the hatchet? After all, he would have become your brother-in-law. It's a great pity he took it into his head to bolt. . . . It makes things look bad for him. I may as well admit to you that I have a warrant for his arrest. What possible reason could he have had, if he is not guilty, for disappearing the way he did, and going to ground in the marshes?"

The cigarettes were dwindling fast. From time to time, a heavy footfall could be heard in the street, someone on his way to the Hôtel du Port for a game of cards.

And the "grilling" went on and on. Occasionally, when his back was turned, Maigret permitted himself to look as disheartened as he felt. He knew it could go on for hours. He had had to deal with all sorts in his time, con men, bamboozlers, masters of repartee.

The most celebrated interrogation in which he had ever taken part at the Quai des Orfèvres had lasted twenty-seven hours. There had been three of them working in relays to ensure that the suspect would not be allowed a minute's respite.

But he could not remember ever having encountered a more unresponsive lump of a man than Albert Forlacroix.

"Marcel is an only child, is he not? And his mother is a widow? Has she any savings? I only ask because, if he should be convicted, that poor woman's life . . ."

"You needn't worry about her. She's far better off than most people in l'Aiguillon."

"I'm relieved to hear it. Because, the more I think about it . . . See here! Would you like me to tell you, just between the two of us, what really happened? If you'll just give me a moment, I have a phone call to make. . . . It had almost slipped my mind, and that might have had serious consequences. . . . Hello, mademoiselle . . . Yes, it's I. . . . About those chocolates I promised you . . . Yes, of course, you did say you preferred marrons glacés. . . . Well, I am becoming more indebted to you all the time. . . . I know it's after hours. . . . But I'd be obliged if you would put me through to Nantes. . . . The Flying Squad, yes . . . Thanks, mademoiselle . . ."

Back to work! It would never do to let Forlacroix off the hook. The pressure must be kept up.

"At first, it was all just a bit of a lark to him, which is understandable enough, at his age. . . . At that stage, the fact that your sister was not quite like other girls didn't worry him all that much. . . . But then he fell in love with her. . . . He began to think seriously about marriage. . . . Didn't he say anything to you at about that time?"

"We weren't on speaking terms."

"Sorry! I was forgetting. But, seeing that he spoke to your father, I thought he just might have gone to see you, too, to explain that you had got hold of the wrong end of the stick, and that, in fact, his intentions were honorable. Oh, well, if you tell me that he didn't . . . Hello . . . Yes . . . Maigret speaking. . . . Look here, I wonder if you could do me a favor. . . . Do you have the address of Doctor Janin's housekeeper? . . . Good . . . Listen . . . I know it's a bit irregular. . . . You'll have to get her consent; otherwise I'll have to wait until tomorrow, to get a summons from the Examining Magistrate. . . . I'd like her brought to me here. . . . Tonight, yes . . . It's only about twelve kilometers. . . . Where? I'll probably still be here, at the town hall. . . . No, don't say anything to her. . . . Thanks."

He hung up, and, assuming his most cordial manner, continued:

"I'm so sorry. . . . Just a small matter that I had overlooked . . . In all probability, Marcel will very shortly be found and

128

apprehended by the police. After all, it's inevitable. The marshes are not the desert. . . . Well, anyway, to get back to my idea . . . Marcel is contemplating marriage. His mother, we can assume, uses all her powers to dissuade him from marrying a mentally subnormal girl. He himself, although very much in love, feels a little uneasy. . . ."

It was hot enough in the room, goodness knows, with the stove roaring away. But was it only because of the heat that Forlacroix's forehead was beaded with perspiration?

"It is at this point that he remembers that one of his old shipmates aboard the *Vengeur* has set up in practice as a doctor in Nantes. He goes to see him. He asks his advice. Janin cannot give an opinion without seeing the girl. They decide that the best course would be for the doctor to visit her here, and examine her. . . ."

Albert stubbed out his cigarette on the heel of his boot, and lit another.

"You must admit that it makes sense, psychologically. . . . Of course, I don't know your former friend Airaud as well as you do. But he is, first and foremost, a peasant. And that means that he is by nature cautious. . . . He wishes to get married, but, at the same time, he would like to be assured that his future wife's mental disorder is not quite hopeless. . . . How does that strike you?"

"I don't know," retorted Albert drily.

"Drink up your wine. . . . Are you still not hungry? In my opinion—I may be wrong, of course—in my opinion Marcel lacked the courage to raise the question with your father. . . . In other words, to put it bluntly, the Judge had agreed to let him have his daughter, but only on the terms that he take her as he found her. . . . And, besides, if she had been a normal, healthy girl, he would probably not have consented to her marrying a mussel-gatherer."

And Maigret, quite deliberately, assumed a sly expression, and uttered a coarse laugh, like a salesman telling a dirty joke.

"Can't you just see our friend Airaud saying to his future father-in-law: 'Agreed! I'm very much obliged to you. I'll take your daughter, but only subject to a favorable expert opinion.'?"

Albert looked at him with loathing, but the Chief Superintendent turned a blind eye.

"It was therefore necessary to arrange to have the girl examined without her father's knowledge. . . . And that, in my opinion, is the reason it was decided that this should take place on a Tuesday. Every Tuesday night, Forlacroix entertained his friends in the library on the ground floor. They could be relied on to remain there for hours, talking in loud voices, drinking and laughing, with never an inkling of what was going on upstairs. . . . There's just one thing that bothers me, Albert. . . . You don't mind if I call you Albert? Yes, just one thing bothers me . . . I know Janin was an eccentric, and, to put it bluntly, a bit of a rebel. Still, all doctors are bound by strict rules of medical ethics. . . .

"Let's go through the train of events as they occurred, and then see if you don't agree that there is something that doesn't quite fit. . . ."

He, too, was feeling the heat. He mopped his face, and filled his pipe. At times like these, he felt something of the strain experienced by a music-hall entertainer who must, at all costs, retain control of his audience and keep them breathless, on the edge of their seats.

He had an audience of only one. But what a rotten audience! Hostile, contemptuous, and unco-operative from start to finish.

"Listen to me, young man. . . . Janin got off at the bus stop. Marcel must have arranged to meet him somewhere not far from the Hôtel du Port. He was anxious that no one know of the doctor's visit. . . .

"Why did Janin decide to stop at the hotel, and tell them that he would be back for dinner?

"Anyway, having done so, he left. He met Marcel. It was too soon to go to the Judge's house. His guests had not yet arrived. It would not be possible to see the girl alone until nine o'clock at the earliest.

"Tell me, where do you think those two men went in the interval? It was raining. I can't somehow see them walking in the dark for hours on end. And besides, if they had done so, someone in the village would surely have seen them. . . .

"And, what's more, they had a meal somewhere. At least Janin did. We know that for certain. Although the information is confidential, I see no harm in telling you that the autopsy revealed the remains of a fairly substantial meal in the dead man's stomach.

"So the two of them ate a hearty meal. Where did they get it? Tell me that."

And Maigret, who had been pacing up and down, stopped for a moment, and gave Albert a hefty thump on the back.

"And that's not the end of it, my dear fellow. . . . The guests are now assembled. First, Brénéol and his wife and daughter, and then the Marsacs. The time has come. All that remains is to gain access to your sister Lise's bedroom, on the second floor. This presented no problem to Marcel, who made quite a habit of scaling the wall.

"As for Doctor Janin, eccentric though he was, climbing walls must have been a new experience for him. . . .

"And yet, how else could he have got in?

"Was Marcel there with him, I wonder?

"Be that as it may, it seems fairly certain that the murder took place about midnight. We have your evidence for that."

"My evidence?"

"Yes, yours, boy. Have you forgotten your statement, which, I should point out, was confirmed in every particular by the Judge? At about midnight, having seen his guests off, the Judge went upstairs, and found you sitting on the top step."

Silence. Maigret refilled his pipe and put some more coal on the fire.

"By the way, why, having broken off relations with the Judge, did you retain your key to the house?"

"So that I could visit my sister."

"Did you see her that night?"

"No!"

"And you heard not a sound, from either bedroom or the fruit loft, although you were almost resting your back against the door? That's right, isn't it? Which is why I say that by then it must have been all over."

He filled a wine glass to the brim, gulped it down, and wiped his mouth.

"That seems to put Judge Forlacroix in the clear, but he's out of the picture anyway. How long had you been in the house when the visitors left? Not very long, I daresay, because you would know what time they usually dispersed?

"Five or ten minutes."

"Five or ten minutes . . . Now, they were playing bridge, and in bridge one player is always dummy. So that sometime in the course of the evening, when he himself was dummy, Forlacroix might well have availed himself of the opportunity of going upstairs to see that everything was all right. . . . He stumbled upon a man who was a stranger to him. He picked up a hammer that had been left lying about. . . . He struck. . . ."

"What are you getting at?" grumbled Albert Forlacroix.

132

"Nothing. I'm just thinking aloud. . . . I've been wanting to exchange ideas with you about all this for a long time. One question in particular springs to mind: did Marcel Airaud enter the house at the same time as the doctor?"

"Are you asking me?"

"No, of course not! How could you possibly know? He may have come in with him in order to take part in the consultation. On the other hand, he may simply have looked in briefly to prepare your sister for the doctor's visit. After all, she was rational enough most of the time. You see, my dear boy, we have to consider all the various alternatives.

"If Airaud and Janin arrived together, it's not inconceivable that they may have had words. Supposing, for instance, that Janin says to him:

" 'You can't possibly marry this girl.'

"He loves her. He has asked for advice, but, who knows? When he actually learns the truth . . .

"There is also the possibility that your sister herself may have . . ."

"Are you suggesting that my sister would be capable . . . ?"

"Calm down! I repeat, I'm just thinking aloud. Every possibility has to be taken into account. Janin examines her, and asks her a great many searching, perhaps even indiscreet questions, such as every doctor feels he has the right to ask. . . .

"All this, plus fear that the doctor might persuade Marcel not to marry her, brings on an attack. . . ."

Phew! He could feel that his cheeks were flushed and his eyes feverish.

"Which is why it would be interesting to know whether Marcel was in the house or waiting outside. Naturally, the fact of his having bolted tells against him. It's not the way you'd expect anyone to behave who had nothing to hide. . . . Unless . . ."

133

He paused, apparently deep in thought, then, once again, he thumped the young man on the back.

"Yes, indeed . . . He'll have a lot to answer for, when we catch him. . . . Let's suppose he stayed outside. He waits. His friend does not return. Much later, he scales the wall, climbs into the fruit loft, and finds the doctor's body. He jumps to the conclusion that Lise has killed him. . . .

"Inquiries are started. He is afraid that suspicion will fall on her. He loves her. Therefore, in order to divert suspicion from his future wife, he pretends to run away. . . .

"It's one way of gaining time, in the hope that the case may ultimately be shelved. What do you say?"

"I have nothing to say."

"Obviously, you have no idea where Marcel could possibly be hiding. . . . No, wait, don't answer now. . . . You were once his friend. He was about to become your brother-in-law. No one could blame you for being reluctant to hand him over to the law. As I say, from the point of view of common human-ity, no one could blame you; though, of course, speaking from the police point of view, you would be committing an offense. Do you understand? Let us suppose that you saw Marcel after he went into hiding, but did not report the fact—it's merely a supposition . . . He may just as easily still be on the run—it would be difficult not to draw certain conclusions."

"What conclusions?" asked Albert slowly, uncrossing his legs and recrossing them the other way. And, as he did so, the ash fell from his cigarette onto his jacket.

"It might be concluded, for instance, that you, too, were anxious to shield your sister. . . . You say you had been on the landing for five or ten minutes, but we have only your word for that. You didn't set foot in the bar that night, did you?"

"Not after nine o'clock."

"You undoubtedly possess a key to your sister's bedroom.

You admitted as much yourself, when you said that you had kept your front-door key in order to be able to visit her. The front-door key would have served no purpose if, when you got inside . . . But I assume you must have mislaid this second key, since, on the night in question, you broke open the door with your shoulder, as I saw for myself. On the other hand, perhaps you forgot about the key in the heat of the moment. Or were you trying to put me off the scent?"

Silence. The young man, staring down at the dusty floor, seemed deep in thought. At length, having come to a decision, he looked up.

"Is this an official interrogation?"

"It's whatever you want it to be."

"Do I have to answer?"

"No."

"In that case, I have nothing to say."

And he stubbed out his cigarette on the sole of his boot.

Maigret wandered around the room a couple of times, picked up the wine bottle, only to find that it was empty, and began turning the handle of the telephone.

"Oh, good. You're still up, mademoiselle. . . . Would you put me through to the Hôtel du Port? . . . Thanks . . . Hello, is that you, Thérèse? . . . Get me Inspector Méjat, there's a good girl. . . . Méjat . . . Listen, dear boy. . . . I want you to go to Albert Forlacroix's place. . . .

"At the end of the back yard you'll find a sort of shed. There's a man in there asleep on a mattress. . . . No, I don't think he's dangerous. . . . Be careful, just the same. . . . Yes, you'd better handcuff him. You might as well be on the safe side. And bring him here to me. . . . That's right. . . . Forla- croix . . . He won't object, no. . . . He's right here. I have his consent."

Maigret hung up with a smile.

"Inspector Méjat was afraid that you might complain about unlawful entry.... Of course, we have no right, especially in the middle of the night, and without a warrant.... Cigarette? No hard feelings, I trust? If I were making the arrest, I doubt if I would be able to resist helping myself to one of those delicious-looking sausages you have hanging over the fireplace...."

Then, very kindly:

"When was it you slaughtered the pig?"

10

Detective Didine

•

During the next few minutes, Maigret behaved as if he had forgotten his companion. First, he took his watch out of his pocket, wound it slowly and deliberately, detached it from its chain, and laid it on the table, with the implication that, from now on, he would be keeping a watchful eye on the time.

Then he waited. Albert Forlacroix did not stir. He did not heave a sigh. Yet he must have been uncomfortable on that hard little chair. He must surely have been repressing a desire to fidget, or perhaps scratch his cheek or his nose, or cross and uncross his legs. But, because Maigret was visibly disciplining himself to remain absolutely still, he, too, was fiercely determined not to move a muscle.

The Chief Superintendent was ostensibly absorbed in contemplation of the stove, and, from where he was sitting, Forlacroix could not see his face, and so was unaware that his lips were twitching in a fleeting, almost mischievous smile.

Well, what did all these ploys amount to? They were no more than tricks of the trade, designed to undermine a fellow's confidence.

Footsteps outside. With quiet deliberation, Maigret went

across to open the door. Marcel Airaud stood in the doorway, wearing handcuffs. Beside him, puffed up with self-importance, was Méjat, holding him by the wrist. They were followed by a policeman, dimly to be discerned in the shadows.

Airaud did not appear distressed. He was blinking, but only because he was dazzled by the light. He remained standing, whereas Forlacroix made no attempt to leave his seat.

"Take this one next door, will you?" said Maigret to the Inspector, pointing to Albert.

"Next door" was the ballroom, with its white walls, paper festoons hanging from the ceiling, and benches along the walls for the chaperones. The two rooms were divided by a glass door.

"Sit down, Airaud. I'll be with you in a minute."

But the young man chose to remain standing. Maigret gave his orders, instructing the policeman to take charge of Forlacroix, and sending Méjat out to fetch sandwiches and beer.

All this was done as though in slow motion. Both Forlacroix and Airaud must have been somewhat baffled by the Chief Superintendent's manner of going about things. And yet both by now must have realized that they were well and truly trapped.

Did Airaud have a sense of humor? It certainly looked like it. He seemed not in the least cowed by the Chief Superintendent's crushing imperturbability. As he watched all his comings and goings, a faint smile played about his lips.

On the other side of the glass door, Forlacroix was sitting on a bench, with his back against the wall, and his legs stretched out. The policeman, taking his duties very seriously, was sitting opposite, his gaze fixed unwaveringly on his face.

"How long have you been in hiding at your friend Albert's place?" Maigret asked abruptly, staring into space.

The sound of his own voice had an immediate and curious effect upon Maigret. It persuaded him that he was wasting his time. He paused for a moment, then turned to the prisoner.

"Am I under arrest?" asked the young man, glancing down at the handcuffs.

"I have here a warrant for your arrest, signed by the Examining Magistrate."

"In that case I refuse to be questioned except by the Examining Magistrate, in the presence of my lawyer."

Maigret, not in the least surprised, looked him up and down.

There was a knock at the door.

"Come in!" called out Maigret, and Méjat appeared with an armful of small packages.

As he was laying out the food on the table—pâté, ham, bread, and small cans of beer—Méjat attempted to whisper something in Maigret's ear.

"Speak up!" ordered Maigret grumpily.

"I was trying to tell you that Thérèse is outside in the forecourt. . . . I fancy she knows something is going on. . . . As soon as she saw me, she asked me if he'd been arrested."

Maigret shrugged, made himself a sandwich, poured himself a glass of beer, and once again looked Airaud up and down. He was by now quite certain that he would get nowhere by piling on the pressure.

"Take him next door, Méjat. Tell the policeman to see that they don't talk to one another. . . . As for you, I want you back in here. . . ."

He paced up and down. He ate. He grumbled to himself. He hunched his shoulders. Every time he passed the door, he could see them sitting on their bench in the spacious white room, and the policeman, with knitted brows, keeping a sharp eye on them.

"How goes it, Chief?" asked Méjat as he came back into the room.

The Chief Superintendent silenced him with a look. He was still unfamiliar with Maigret's ways. He did not know how to behave.

Maigret just went on eating, stuffing unwieldy lumps of food into his mouth, and, chewing away, stumped across to the door and stood gazing at his two caged beasts through the glass.

Suddenly he swung around.

"Go and fetch Didine here."

"I won't have far to go. When I came in just now, she was keeping watch only about ten yards away."

"Bring her in."

"What about Thérèse?"

"Did I say anything about Thérèse?"

It was not long before the little old woman could be seen hurrying across the ballroom, pausing only to gaze with undisguised satisfaction at the two young men. She seemed especially enchanted by the sight of Marcel Airaud's glinting handcuffs.

"Come in, Didine. I need your help."

"Well, you finally caught up with that fellow, I see. . . ."

"Take a seat, Didine. I won't offer you a beer. . . . Or would you care for a glass?"

"I don't like beer. . . . So you've arrested him at long last."

"Listen carefully, Didine. Take your time about answering. It's very important. . . . For heaven's sake, Méjat, sit down or take yourself for a walk, or something, but do stop gawping at me like an idiot. . . . Now, Didine . . . suppose someone were to announce to you, in the middle of the afternoon, that they intended coming to dinner with you that night . . . someone from the town. . . . What would you do?"

Anyone not familiar with Didine's character might have

expected her to give a start of surprise at such an unexpected question. But this was far from being her reaction. On the contrary, she became very quiet, and her features seemed to sharpen with the effort of concentration. Maigret need not have troubled himself to urge her to take her time. She would have done so in any case.

"What sort of person?" she asked.

"A person of some standing."

"And it would be sprung on me in the middle of the afternoon? What time, exactly?"

"Let's say between half past four and five."

The three men on the other side of the glass door, Airaud, Forlacroix, and the policeman, were all looking in at them, but they were now situated as Maigret had been earlier in the day. They could see the speakers' lips moving, but could hear only a confused murmur of voices.

"I don't know if you have quite got my drift. You are familiar with the daily habits of all the people hereabouts, and you know what supplies are available in l'Aiguillon. Who better than you to tell me where one would go for food at any particular hour of the day?"

"It would be too late to kill a chicken. It wouldn't be tender in time," she murmured, as if to herself. "Not to mention the time it takes to draw and pluck it . . . Had you any particular day of the week in mind, Chief Superintendent?"

Méjat looked absolutely dumbfounded. As to Maigret, he did not permit himself so much as a ghost of a smile.

"A Tuesday."

"Ah! I think I see what you're getting at. . . . You're thinking of that particular Tuesday, aren't you? You'd think it was done on purpose to make things difficult. . . . I remarked on the fact to my husband. I said to him the man must have got a meal somewhere. . . . Now, he didn't dine at the hotel, or at the Judge's house. . . ."

"You haven't answered my question, Didine. If it had been you, what would you have given him on a Tuesday?"

"Not meat . . . Here in the village, Monday is slaughter day. The meat is too fresh to eat on Tuesday. It would be very tough. . . . Just a minute, though! What was the state of the tide on that Tuesday? High tide would have been about eight at night, wouldn't it? . . . So Polyte would have been at home. . . . In that case, if it had been me, I would have nipped across to Polyte's place. He always goes out with his nets on the morning tide. So he would have been home by midday. . . . If he had a nice big fish . . ."

"Where does Polyte live?"

"He won't be home now. . . . He'll be at the bar. . . . Not the Hôtel du Port; the one opposite."

"You hear that, Méjat?"

Méjat did not need to be told. He went out. The old woman went on.

"When Polyte has a couple of good sole or a plump Saint-Pierre, you have a first course fit for anyone. And provided there's a bite of ham in the house . . . But . . . hold on, Chief Superintendent. . . . Polyte isn't the only one. . . . If you happen to like plovers, there's always old Père Rouillon, who goes out with his gun every morning. . . ."

The three men were still there on the other side of the glass door. Forlacroix's expression was somber. Airaud, in spite of his handcuffs, was puffing at a cigarette, his eyes screwed up on account of the smoke.

"Only, to cook plovers, you need . . ."

Méjat strode across the ballroom, accompanied by a scraggy fisherman with a pointed nose and a brick-red complexion. On seeing Airaud, the man stopped, and stared at him in amazement.

"Well! I'll be damned! So you're back, are you?"

142

"Come in here, will you?" interposed Maigret. "Is your name Polyte?"

The fisherman peered uneasily at the old woman. What on earth could she have been saying about him to cause him to be sent for like this?

"Well now, Polyte . . . do you remember last Tuesday?"

"Tuesday?" he repeated, looking completely at sea.

"The day of the fair at Saint-Michel," prompted Didine. "The day when there was a high tide of three foot six."

"What about it? What am I supposed to have done that day?"

"One thing's for sure: you spent most of it tippling as usual," murmured Didine, unable to resist the temptation to put her oar in again.

"Where were you that afternoon?"

It was Didine, ever alert, who replied:

"In the bar, where else? He'd set up a bed there if he could. Isn't that so, Polyte?"

"What I would like to know is whether anyone came to see you that afternoon, wanting to buy something special in the fish line."

Forlacroix sat watchful and gloomy in the next room. Polyte reflected, then turned to Didine as if seeking guidance.

"The day when there was a high tide of three foot six? You don't happen to remember, do you?" he asked with disarming candor.

Then suddenly he swung around to face the glass door and clapped his hand to his forehead, whereupon Didine's face lit up with a triumphant smile.

"It was Albert who came!" he exclaimed. "I remember he was in a great hurry. I was playing cards with Deveaud and Fraigne. 'I won't keep you a moment,' I said. Then, seeing that he was getting impatient, I told him he could help himself to sole from the boat."

"How many sole?"

"I don't even know how many he took. I told him to help himself. . . . We haven't settled up for them yet."

"That's all I want to know. You may go now. . . . Oh, by the way, Didine, where does Albert Forlacroix's housekeeper live?"

"As it happens, she's *his* daughter."

"Polyte's?"

"Yes. But she doesn't live with her father. If you want to see her, you'll have to be quick about it, because she turns in very early. Especially now, when, just for a change, she's in the family way. She has one a year. She's got quite a little colony. . . ."

"Méjat! Go and get her, will you? But don't hustle her, mind."

His pulse was beginning to race. Polyte stood hesitating for a moment in the doorway, waiting for permission to leave, then he went off with the Inspector to show him the way to his daughter's cottage.

"It's a wonder the men aren't put off by her. Wait till you see her! And I bet she'll have cleaned herself up a bit before coming here. As for me, if I had to eat anything touched by her . . ."

She saw to her surprise that the Chief Superintendent was standing motionless in the middle of the room, seemingly deaf and blind to everything around him. He had just been struck by a thought. Abruptly, he strode across the room and seized the telephone.

"I hope I didn't get you out of bed, mademoiselle? . . . Get me the Albert Premier Nursing Home in La Roche-sur-Yon, will you, please? The number is four one. Keep on ringing until they answer. There must be at least one night nurse on duty. . . . Yes, thanks . . ."

He had forgotten Didine, when he heard her ask, in her usual quiet way:

"Do you think Marcel is the one? If you want my opinion, knowing both of them as I do . . ."

"Quiet!" he barked, sounding like a man in a temper.

He could not take his eyes off the telephone. For hours, for days now, he had been searching . . .

"Hello. Is that the Albert Premier Nursing Home? . . . Who is speaking? . . . Tell me, mademoiselle, is the Superintendent still there? . . . He's at home, you say? . . . Could you transfer me to his number? . . .

His cheeks were flushed, and he was chewing on the stem of his pipe. He gazed abstractedly at Didine, as if he did not know who she was.

"Hello. Is that you, doctor? . . . Did I disturb your dinner? . . . I'm so sorry. . . . Chief Superintendent Maigret, yes . . . I just wanted to ask you . . . You have examined her, of course? . . . What's that? . . . Her condition is worse than you had thought? . . . But it's not about that I'm calling you. I wanted to ask you if you'd found anything you weren't expecting. . . . Yes . . . What? . . . Are you absolutely sure? . . . Three months? . . . Thanks, doctor . . . Yes, of course, I will await your official report. . . . Has she settled down all right? . . . Thanks . . . And, once again, my apologies for having disturbed you."

His nerves were on edge. When he realized that Didine was still sitting there, in her chair, he said:

"Now then, Didine, run along home, there's a good soul. . . . You have been most helpful, but I don't need you any more for the present."

With great reluctance, she stood up, but she was not quite ready to leave yet.

"I bet I can guess what he told you."

"Good for you! Now be off with you. . . . If you really feel you must, you can wait in the next room, but . . ."

"She's pregnant, isn't she?"

He could scarcely believe his ears. Her perspicacity was really almost frightening.

"I haven't time to talk to you now. . . . Go! And, above all, keep your mouth shut!"

He opened the door. Just as he was about to shut it again, Méjat reappeared, accompanied by a young woman with filthy hair hanging down to her shoulders.

"She didn't want to come at first, because she was getting ready for bed."

At this point, there was a slight stir in the room beyond. At the sight of his housekeeper, Forlacroix had half risen from his bench, as if about to intervene. But unfortunately the policeman laid a restraining hand on his arm. This was enough to recall to him where he was, and he resumed his seat.

"Good! Come in here a minute. . . . I just want to ask you a couple of questions. . . . What time do you finish work at Albert Forlacroix's?"

"It varies. Sometimes it's three o'clock, sometimes four."

"Do you get his evening meal ready for him?"

"I don't do any meals for him. He does his own cooking. He likes cooking."

She sounded sarcastic and somewhat contemptuous.

"You do his washing up, I presume?"

"Oh, yes, I do the dirty work; that's all I'm fit for. . . . And there's plenty of dirty work to be done in that house! When a man is spruced up to go out, that's one thing, but when it comes to cleaning the house . . ."

"Does he entertain much?"

"Who?"

"Your employer?"

"Never. Who is there for him to entertain?"

146

"Was there ever an occasion when you found more washing up than usual waiting for you when you arrived in the morning?"

"As a matter of fact, I did, one day last week!"

"Would that have been on Wednesday?"

"It might have been Wednesday.... And there was ash all over the place. Someone had been smoking cigars."

"You don't happen to know who his visitors were?"

She turned toward the glass door and, clasping her stomach with both hands, retorted without malice:

"Why don't you ask him?"

"Thank you. You may go home to bed now."

"Is he the one who did it?"

She was neither shocked nor alarmed at the thought. Indeed, she was not even particularly curious, as her next words showed.

"I only ask because I want to know whether I'm expected to go to work as usual tomorrow."

Voices could be heard in the street, beyond the gate of the town hall. Word had got around that something was afoot. A small crowd had gathered. All eyes were turned toward the cream-colored blinds, across which shadows moved from time to time, especially the bulky shadow of Maigret, and of his pipe, which, seen from a particular angle, appeared greatly magnified, so that the bowl seemed almost as large as his head.

"I think they've arrested the pair of them!" announced Polyte's daughter, in reply to eager questioning, when she emerged from the town hall.

She was dropping with sleep, and it was not long before her clogs could be heard receding into the distance on the icy cobblestones. The door opened. Méjat peered out into the darkness, trying to identify the faces in the street.

147

"Is Thérèse still there?" he asked.

A shadowy figure moved forward into the light.

"I'm here. What is it?"

"Come inside. The Chief Superintendent wants a word with you."

She glanced at Marcel in passing, but did not utter a word.

"Come in, Thérèse. There's nothing to be afraid of. There's just one thing I wanted to ask you. . . . Did you know that Lise Forlacroix was pregnant?"

Abruptly she swung around to face the glass door, as if about to hurl herself upon Airaud, who looked utterly bewildered, having not the least idea of what was going on.

Then, thinking better of it, she protested:

"It's a lie! You're just scaring me."

"I give you my word, Thérèse, that Lise Forlacroix is three months pregnant."

"So that's why . . ." she murmured to herself.

"Why what?"

"Why he wanted to marry her."

"So you admit that he wanted to marry her? But he didn't tell you the reason, is that it? Well, now you know. You know that . . ."

"Well, didn't I have a child by him? I'm every bit as good as the Judge's daughter, aren't I? Did he ever offer to marry me?"

It must have been an odd experience, to watch her through the glass door. Her fury was plain to see, but it would be hard to guess what had caused it.

"Come to think of it, only that very night . . ."

"Yes? What was it you said to him that night?"

"I told him that if he married her I would turn up at the church with my son and make a scene."

148

"Let's get this straight. You saw him that Tuesday night, did you? Where?"

She hesitated for an instant, then shrugged.

"In the street."

"What time was this?"

"Just before midnight, I think."

"Are you saying you ran into him on the street?"

Once more she turned toward the glass door, and said viciously:

"I'll tell you the whole story. Who cares? . . . I was getting ready for bed around ten, when I saw a light in her ladyship's bedroom. . . ."

"Are you sure it was her bedroom, and not the fruit loft?"

"It was her bedroom."

"You're quite sure you know which is which?"

She laughed sarcastically.

"Oh, yes, I'm sure. . . . I've spied on the pair of them often enough! I tried to get to sleep, but I couldn't. So I got up again, and decided to go and wait for him outside."

"What for?"

"The same as usual," she admitted wearily.

"Did you threaten him with anything worse than making a scene in the church?"

"I told him I'd go to his house and kill myself."

"And would you have done that?"

"I really don't know. . . . I crept out without making a sound. It was raining. So hard that I had to pull my coat up over my head. I wondered if I would have to wait long. . . . If he'd been too long coming, I think I might have climbed up there myself."

"What happened then?"

"I walked about, talking to myself, as I often do. I wasn't looking where I was going. . . . The streets were deserted. . . .

Then, suddenly, I bumped into someone. It was him. I was so taken aback, I cried out. . . ."

"Where was this?"

"Close to the wall, at the back of the Judge's house."

"What was he doing? Leaving the house?"

"No. He wasn't doing anything. He seemed to be keeping watch. I asked him what he was waiting for."

"What did he say?"

"Nothing. He grabbed hold of my wrists and twisted them. He was furious. 'If ever I catch you spying on me again,' he growled, 'I don't know what I'll do.' "

"What time was this?"

"Not far short of midnight, as I told you. Perhaps a little later . . ."

"Was the light still on in the bedroom?"

"I don't know. I couldn't see from there because of the wall. He shrieked at me, 'Go back to bed, you bitch. Do you hear me? And if ever' . . . I'd never seen him so angry."

Another glance at the glass door. In the ballroom beyond, Airaud seemed quite unperturbed. The policeman must have given him another cigarette, since he was holding one, very awkwardly, on account of the handcuffs.

"Would you mind waiting next door, Thérèse? I may be needing you again."

He shut the door behind her, and then heard a voice. It was Méjat, saying:

"Hey, Chief . . . it seems to me . . ."

"What?"

"It seems to me that . . . that . . ."

Poor fellow! He only wanted to be kind, to congratulate Maigret on getting results. And all he got for his pains was a savage glare.

"Well? Out with it! Say what you have to say! Maybe you

can tell me how we set about getting the necessary evidence, is that it? Oh, well, go and get me some beer, there's a good fellow. . . . No, wait. . . . Bring some brandy instead, or Calvados or rum—it doesn't matter which. What time is it?"

It was midnight. Outside, the crowd had dwindled to three. These were tramping up and down, hoping that there would be some definite news before long.

11

The Doctor's Housekeeper

•

The purr of a car engine, the grinding of brakes, the banging of doors, followed immediately by the appearance in the ballroom of two police inspectors, accompanied by a woman in her thirties, who looked thoroughly dazed.

"Sorry, Chief Superintendent. We had a flat tire on the way, and we couldn't get the jack to work. So we . . ."

"Is this she?" asked Maigret, subjecting the young woman to a long scrutiny. She appeared utterly bewildered, looking wildly about her and seeing nothing.

"She didn't want to come, on account of her sister-in-law, who is ill. We had to promise to get her back tonight."

Suddenly the girl caught sight of the handcuffs, and gave a little stifled shriek.

"Do you recognize him?" asked the Chief Superintendent. "Take a good look at him. . . . Now, tell me, did that man there, to your knowledge, recently call to see your employer?"

"I recognize them," she replied, recovering her self-possession.

"You . . . What was that you said? You recognize *them?*"

"Certainly! I recognize both of them, which isn't surprising, seeing that they were together."

"And they both went to see the doctor in his office?"

"Both of them. Not right away, because the doctor was out. I suggested that they come back the following day, but they preferred to wait, and they were there in the waiting room for over two hours."

"Well, that's that," growled Maigret. "I needn't trouble you any further."

"Are we to take her back home?" asked one of the inspectors, feeling somewhat let down.

"If you like . . . Wait, though. Here comes Méjat with something to drink. . . . Only I don't know if there are enough glasses. . . ."

At this Didine, still there and ever obliging, stood up and touched the Chief Superintendent on the arm.

"In the cupboard," she whispered.

"What do you mean, 'in the cupboard'?"

"The glasses. They're always kept there, for council meetings. Would you like me to give them a wipe?"

There was nothing she did not know! She saw all there was to see, and heard all there was to hear!

The policemen clinked glasses. Noticing that the doctor's housekeeper was shivering, Maigret poured a small drink for her as well, but all it did was to send her off into a paroxysm of coughing.

Maigret's head was buzzing. He was so obviously, visibly tense that Méjat seemed a little anxious on his account. All of a sudden, Maigret strode over to the glass door and opened it. The inspectors had gone. The car was revving up outside.

"Come here, you!" he barked, addressing Airaud with surprising roughness. "Get those handcuffs off him, Méjat. . . . They make him look ridiculous. . . . Come in. Shut the door, Méjat. And as for you, I don't want any more of your nonsense, do you hear? I've had just about enough. Yes, I've had enough."

It was so unexpected that Airaud looked completely nonplussed.

"I suppose you think you've been very clever, and that you're very pleased with yourself. Isn't that so? Of course, it is! Just take a look at yourself in the mirror! And for heaven's sake stop shifting from one foot to another like a dancing bear. . . . What did your father do for a living?"

So unprepared was he for the question that Airaud, in spite of his determination to remain silent, could not stop himself from murmuring:

"He was a mussel-gatherer."

"And you, too, are a mussel-gatherer. To you, the daughter of a judge must have seemed a great prize. Isn't that so? You couldn't see, could you, what a fool you were making of yourself, or that you were the laughingstock of the village? When did you and Forlacroix bury the hatchet?"

A resentful silence.

"Have it your own way! Don't answer. . . . It makes you look more of a fool than ever."

By now Maigret was so carried away that he was shouting at the top of his voice, so that, even if his actual words could not be heard through the glass door, it was impossible not to catch the drift of what he was saying.

And the Chief Superintendent, still shouting, still pacing up and down, still chewing on the stem of his pipe, poured himself a drink with such frenzied abandon that Méjat's heart was in his mouth.

"Silence at all costs! Anyway, you're so stupid, I don't suppose there's much that you could tell me. I should have thought that business with Thérèse would have taught you a lesson. But you were going to marry her, weren't you? Every-

154

one knew that. . . . Only everyone knew something that you didn't know. . . ."

"I did know."

"What did you know?"

"That she was going with other men."

"Right! And you didn't marry her. That was something. . . . You realized that you were being taken for a ride. . . . But Thérèse was only a chambermaid in a hotel, the child of a woman who sold fish off a barrow. . . . Whereas the other one . . ."

Airaud's expression hardened, and Maigret was not so carried away that he failed to see the young man clench his hefty fists. For an instant he turned his head away—perhaps to hide a smile? He took a long drink from his glass, possibly because he was having some difficulty in keeping up his hectoring tone.

"Our young gentleman was very proud of himself. He was the acknowledged lover of Mademoiselle Forlacroix, who played the piano and whose father was a judge."

"Listen, Chief Superintendent . . ."

"Shut up! You have nothing to say in the absence of your lawyer. You told me so yourself. . . . Our young gentleman is in love. Our young gentleman is puffed up with his own importance. But when Papa Forlacroix, who has been lying in wait for him outside the door, invites him into his library, our young gentleman can do no better than stammer like a schoolboy.

" 'Really? You love my daughter? Well, I've nothing against that! She is yours! Take her. Marry her. . . .'

"That's how it went, isn't it? And that great booby, who may be strong enough to kill an ox, but can't see any further than the end of his nose, stammers:

" 'Yes, sir, I'll marry her! Yes, sir, I am a respectable man, and my intentions are honorable.'

155

"Our young friend is so overwhelmed, so transported with joy and pride, that he can't wait to tell someone. He goes to see his old enemy, young Forlacroix, who has threatened times without number to smash his face in. . . .

" 'You don't know me as I really am. I want to marry your sister. Can't we be friends?' "

On the other side of the glass door, Forlacroix, his neck stretched to the uttermost, was straining to hear what was being said, and Didine was perched on the very edge of her seat.

"Well, boy, I have one thing to tell you that will be news to you, which is that you were well and truly had by the pair of them. You still don't know what I'm talking about, is that it? You thought it was because they had recognized your worth that they received you with open arms.

"The only one not taken in was that grand old woman, your mother. . . . And I bet you were livid when she advised you to be careful and not let yourself be carried away. . . .

" 'I promise you, Mother, Lise isn't as mad as people say. Once she's happily settled, and properly looked after . . .'

"Hook, line, and sinker! You poor, silly dupe!"

He looked the young man over from head to foot, then turned to Méjat and winked. The Inspector could not imagine what he meant by it.

"The one glimmer of common sense in this whole affair, I have no doubt, was shown by your mother. What concession could she hope for, poor woman, from a son as stubborn and hot-headed as you?

" 'At least get a doctor to examine her. What if, in spite of all you say, she really is quite mad?'

"At this point, you remembered your former shipmate, Janin. You took Albert along with you, so that he would be left in no doubt as to your good intentions. If, after having examined Lise, the doctor should decide that . . .

"What? That wasn't the way it went? Don't answer! Remember, you have nothing to say, except in the presence of your lawyer, isn't that so?

"Albert, for his part, knew that his sister was pregnant. . . ."

Airaud's response was so sudden and violent that Maigret had no time to duck out of harm's way. Besides, he was probably quite satisfied with the way the situation was developing. Airaud seized him by the lapels of his jacket, and, believe it or not, seemed about to give him a good shaking.

"What's that you said? What's that you said?"

"The doctor of the nursing home will confirm it. . . . You have only to call and ask him. . . . But for the time being . . ."

"Lise is . . ."

"Pregnant. Yes, by God! These things do happen. And that's why the Judge was so amenable, all of a sudden, to the prospect of having a great lout like you for a son-in-law.

"And that's why Albert went with you to Nantes. He was very much on his guard. He didn't relish the idea of his sister, and for that matter himself, becoming the laughing stock of l'Aiguillon.

"There was just one small point that worried me. . . . I simply couldn't see Janin agreeing to shin up a wall in order to visit a patient.

"But, of course, there was no need for that. You couldn't take him home, because that would have meant taking your mother into your confidence, which was the last thing you wanted.

"So the three of you went to Albert's place for dinner. . . . I can even tell you what you had to eat: sole . . .

"You waited until the Judge's guests had arrived and settled down to a game of bridge. The way now being clear, Albert introduced the doctor into the house. He had the key. . . . It was easy enough to creep up to the next floor without making a sound. My suspicions were aroused when, in my presence, he found it necessary to break down the door with his shoulder. Seeing that he had a key to the front door, it was more than likely . . . But that's no concern of yours. He took Doctor Janin to see his sister. He waited outside. . . .

"As for you, good-natured fool that you are, you stayed outside, pacing up and down beside the wall that you had so often climbed."

Maigret turned toward the door, and saw Albert Forlacroix standing close to it, with a threatening expression on his face.

"You had a rotten time of it, one way and another, didn't you? First, there was Thérèse, with her meddling and threats. . . . And, as time went by and the two men didn't come back, you must have wondered what on earth was happening. . . . Well, I'll tell you. . . . Having completed his examination of the girl, Doctor Janin went into the fruit loft, where Albert was waiting. It's not hard to guess what he said. His first words must have been:

" 'But your sister is expecting a child. . . .'

"Then . . . Look at him. . . . No, not the Inspector . . . over there, through the door . . . Look at his face."

Albert Forlacroix's hand was on the doorknob. He was deathly pale, his nostrils were pinched, and there was a peculiar film of moisture on his lips.

"Come in, Forlacroix. I want you to hear this. . . . I'm about to tell what the doctor said to you. He told you that your sister was incurable. He said that you could not honorably marry her off to any normal, decent man, that she ought to be put in a home, and that his duty as a doctor was to . . ."

"It's not true!" exclaimed Albert furiously.

"What isn't true?"

"I didn't kill him. It was my sister. . . ."

His head was thrust forward, as if he was preparing to ram the Chief Superintendent in the chest.

"That's the story you told Marcel when you went out to him alone. Unfortunately for you, however, if Lise had killed the doctor, using the hammer from the fruit loft, it would never have occurred to her to wipe the handle afterward. . . . Do you think she has even so much as heard of fingerprints? No, no, boy. You were the one to strike the blow, in one of your fits of rage. And you'll be having another of them any minute now, if you don't watch out. . . .

"The doctor said that he intended to tell the whole truth to his friend Airaud. . . .

"You protested. You wanted the marriage to take place at all costs. . . .

"And then suddenly you flew into one of your ungovernable rages. . . .

"And do you know—yes, I could swear it—do you know what Doctor Janin must have thought when he saw you coming at him like a thing possessed?

"He must have thought that your sister was not the only mad one in the family, and that . . ."

Albert, his features contorted, his eyes blazing, sprang at Maigret. His harsh breathing seemed to fill the room, but before he could get at the Chief Superintendent, Marcel had grabbed him by the shoulders, and they were both rolling on the floor.

Apparently unconcerned with the outcome, Maigret went across to the table, poured himself a drink, relit his pipe, and mopped his brow.

"Get the handcuffs on him if you can, Méjat. Better to be on the safe side."

It was no easy task. The two men, grappling together, were equally matched in strength. Forlacroix had managed to get Airaud's thumb between his teeth, and he was biting it savagely. Marcel could not stop himself from crying out. One handcuff clicked shut. Méjat could not get a grip on Albert's other hand. Suddenly he lost his head and, in a dazed and clumsy fashion, began pounding Albert with his fists.

Didine's face was pressed against the glass. Her nose was flattened, her eyes sparkling, and her thin lips wreathed in a happy smile.

"How is it going?"

"There you are, Chief. All done."

At long last, the prisoner's other wrist was encircled by a ring of steel.

Marcel Airaud staggered to his feet, his right hand clenched around his bleeding left thumb. He, too, resorted to the bottle of spirits on the table. But instead of drinking from it, he poured some of the contents over his wound. Forlacroix had bitten him to the bone.

The policeman knocked at the door, and opened it a crack.

"Can I be of any use?"

As he spoke, Maigret was gazing from one to another of the people in the two rooms with a dazed expression on his face. He looked at Didine, nodding her head in satisfaction; at Méjat, staring with disgust at his bloodstained hands; at the policeman, peering about him in bewilderment; at Airaud, bandaging his thumb with a checked handkerchief.

Albert Forlacroix raised himself with difficulty, or, rather, struggled into a sitting position where he was on the floor, and remained there in a stupor, his body twitching.

It was so quiet in the room that the steady tick-tock of the watch on the table could clearly be heard. Maigret fastened it back on its chain. The hands stood at ten minutes past two.

"He told me she'd done it, and I believed him," murmured Airaud, staring blankly at his thumb. "That was why, to divert suspicion . . ."

Maigret felt exhausted. It was as if the weight of the world had been lifted off his shoulders.

"See to them, will you, Méjat?"

He went out, relit his pipe, and walked slowly down to the harbor. He could hear the patter of footsteps behind him. The tide was rising. The beams from the lighthouses intersected in the sky. The moon had just risen, and the Judge's house stood out against the night sky, all white, a harsh, glaring, unreal white.

The footsteps had stopped. Two shadowy figures came together at the corner of the street. Didine had rejoined her squint-eyed customs officer, who had been waiting for her there. She was talking to him in an undertone.

"I wonder if they'll chop off his head!" she said, shivering and huddling closer into her shawl.

Presently a door creaked. They had gone indoors. Soon they would be climbing into their high bed, with its voluminous down quilt, and for a long time after, no doubt, they would talk in whispers.

Alone at last, Maigret was surprised to hear himself murmur dreamily:

"Well! That's it!"

It was over. He would probably never return to l'Aiguillon. In time it would recede and diminish in his memory, until it was like one of those miniature landscapes, tiny, but perfect in every detail, that are to be found in glass paperweights. A little world ... People converging on it from all over the country ... The judge sitting beside his fire ... Lise in her bed, her fleshy lips, her gold-flecked eyes, her plump, naked breast ... Constantinesco in the apartment in Versailles, with his daughter studying music at the conservatory ... Old Horace Van Usschen, with those absurdly light trousers of his, and his white cloth cap ... Thérèse, who would find someone to marry her eventually, at whatever cost ... The widow Airaud, already resigned to living alone for the rest of her life, being confronted with her giant of a son ...

He started, suddenly aware of a steady, rhythmic sound in

161

the night. Then he realized that it must be old Bariteau going out to lay his eel traps.

Come to think of it, what was the state of the tide tonight?

Nieul   **January 31, 1940**